YouSophic Publishing

ISBN-10: 0-9796613-4-X
ISBN-13: 978-0-9796613-4-1
Library of Congress Control Number: 2007905828

FIC000000 **FICTION** / General

Author's Note

Today on the radio, I heard what I thought to be a song from Bob Dylan's newest album, recently just came out – though it might not have been. I purposefully didn't listen. Cut myself off from it completely so I wouldn't hear any bit at all. Very reactionary-like. I don't know what that means, but it somehow connects the half million thoughts that have been going through my head as of late. Things always seem to connect. It's the strings. String Theory, Jane. String Theory. We've all got our feet stuck in some membrane that we're living on & many more exist around worlds that may be like ours, or they may be different. Mathematics breaks down & somehow shows the existence of an infinite amount of parallel universes. That sounds like trouble. Oh Jane, we're such different people. Sometimes I get angry, but I always believe you & I don't stay mad for too long. I've been reading Charles Dickens. American Notes. He's British. It's thick writing that bogs you down. I think I've read 14 pages in 2 weeks. Chomping through concrete. I can only read this one page a day. He writes so convincingly. You're sure of everything he says. The most beautiful bullshit, something you'd never once think of to say. Bushes filled with beetles wear bumble B Sox & after a few lines it clicks & you just feel so smart too. Quite remarkable. It energizes me. I'm glad to have started working again. I've never been so motivated to write. I told you that already. I'm hesitant though. I feel like I don't have my mind completely settled on what's worth writing about, worth pointing to & shouting out, but I'm on my way. It's important to know what you are saying first, rub it through shit then go on & hang it outside. I started to read People's History again & I'm now able to do it without getting too down. It'd be to miss the point to feel educated in truth from it, but I find perspective. I'm not sure there is a real truth in history, that's just not how it seems to work. Truth is nearly trivial. It's not much to believe in. There are too many truths. People build up everything based on their own standards far too often & it leads to falsities - no truths. Neutrality is boring, but being introspective & finding where someone might be coming from, be it sadly unheard of, seems to be the closest thing to a true truth —> Truth, Booth, Sleuth. I'm not hardly a serious person. I got called a stoner today & I didn't like that. I've never been stoned. Someone else, whom I'd been talking with for a little while, told me of a girl coming named VA, said she was right up my alley. Those were his words. I looked down at my red striped pants & green & blue ruffled shirt & 'oh that alley', I said. She showed up wearing an army fatigue mini-skirt. I said hello & she chewed her gum at me. I use the word 'seems' a lot because I'm scared to call anything on what of it is readily apparent. I'm wrong all the time. There are secrets about myself that I can't give to anyone else. I learned that from somebody, but I can't tell you who. I came halfway down the stairs to hear another person saying that I've yet to grow up, I'll outgrow this silly writing business, I could never amount to nothing from it, & if he didn't think he'd hate himself for it, he'd sign me up for the military tomorrow!! Who are these strange people? How did I get chosen to be gravitationally hung to them? I am treated as the blue-toothed, cockeyed, upside-down walker, who's known nothing about anything for even one second. Just lightly patted on the head when I come around. Constantly under an attempt to be formed into the slightly-above-average-moneymaker by dull pokes of a point. I don't know who will learn first, me or them. I'm looking for another membrane. That's what this story is about. Membranes, membranes & more membranes. Oh, Jane. I wish I'd written you Girl from the North Country. You & I are stuck in the old days my dear. For only now perhaps, but of course until who knows. I'm sure & gone, hoping to take with me anything that may ail you.

M

It was a very good year. A year for birds to bathe in the rain. Cool, fat drops. If in the years past, one were to have been scraping through life stuck in thirst and burns, all would be quenched that year with a mouth cocked open to the sky. At night the street let go drunk laughter, and through thin walls and open windows those inside were made witness to the deliberate negligence. People were getting together all over the place, never bringing up any matter that could spread a damper on the spirit. Just ordering more beer. Sales on musical instruments soared to an all-time high, and it seemed every little girl in a polka dot dress was able to push Ornette notes through saxophones and play bluegrass on their fiddles. Tramps had been carted out, and the free man was everybody. Workers collected their wage, and bosses dosed out bonuses. Who knows how they finally learned to get along. It was a very good year. Nobody sat on anybody's face. Wading in the ocean was expected, and one could brave dives to its depths in search of treasure, not once having to worry about coming up for air. The leaders of the world had hair on their heads, wore t-shirts to work, and showed no inclination to be involved in something so trivial as politics. Politics was reserved for chess games, claiming shotgun, and underwater air-less mask-less wrestling matches. Even without the fun of a war, people could be entertained, economies sustained. Words that meant one thing the year before didn't mean that anymore, there were new definitions, new words to define, and new experiences to bunch the letters for. The stone cold paranoid could sit easy in their upright chairs. They giggled, and even would stand-up from out of their seat, step from underneath the cover of the roof, and see what the sun thought for the day. Those composing any bit of random form that, be it to oscillate or not, could be conceived of as art, did whatever it was they pleased that year. Ignoring any one convention, and along with it any naysayer who demanded things to be done their way, with their wax and their comb. People cut hair as they pleased. No sort of droid walked the sidewalk in hopes of mingling, nobody fake, every mind in synch and every hand in hold of exactly what they were meant for. A lovely union, a peaceful one. It was a very good year. It was the year after this.

At one of the Fish Kettle's outside tables, an open-ended sort of restaurant and bar on Huntington Street, two friends joined Page on a Saturday afternoon. Page lived on Huntington Street, as did Colander, and while Longwell made residence somewhere else, he spent most of his time on Huntington Street too.

"How come you think that cop's gotta drive around like that?" Page asked.

"Who cares? Cops are always driving around. That's what they do," Longwell responded.

Page put a cigarette in his mouth. Colander hadn't said anything for awhile. Hanging off his seat, Colander's long legs arched the sidewalk and stood over many bricks. Longwell pried a sunflower seed out with his tongue then spit the shell. Page stood up to leave. He took out his lighter, and Colander looked at him in search of a word to say. Longwell stared down the street.

A man who lived in fear of yawning, for he felt it to be the beginnings of throwing-up, walked the sidewalk alone and pale. He crossed in front of a couple coming out of an alley, guilty faced, hand-in-hand. The man of the couple turned back to the woman, and she bashfully smiled before giving a laugh. Glass shards stuck in her hair, and to the bottom of their shoes. A middle aged man, well-dressed and kept, was across the street. He looked to the sky, mouthing something before dropping his letter into the post office slot. Longwell remained quiet, his attention still down the street, his foot resting on its opposite knee. Page lit the cigarette and walked away.

"Hey, did you get the note I left you?"

"Note? No, no note."

"Oh, well I left you one on your car windshield. You didn't see it?" Page asked, putting his hand on Addie's shoulder. She had been waiting in Page's apartment for an hour.

"No, I would never notice a note on the windshield. It probably blew off once I started driving."

"Oh. Alright, well, whatever. It's so nice to see you my darling," Page wrapped his arms around the back of her neck and buried his face into her dark hair.

"Hey, get outta here!" She said laughing and pushing him back.

"Stop it, I'm smelling you."

"Smell yourself."

"I wanna smell you," he said and stuck his nose back in.

"You think you're a sweetheart."

Page removed his jacket and placed it on a hook that stuck from his bedroom door. He took from his pant pockets loose coins, a small notepad, and a pen.

Each item, he tossed onto the bedroom bureau.

"What are you reading?" he asked.

"Rimbaud," she replied and turned the page. "They had to amputate his leg, and he died of the hole they cut being too big."

Page widened his eyes and nodded. He turned from her and ripped the shirt-bottom from out of his pants. Untucked, he looked into the mirror that extended from the bureau. He saw himself and Addie's back to him on the other side of the room. Under his eyes were the dark circles he expected. Her neck was hunched into the book, and her fingers tapping the crest of her head. She read aloud:

> It has been found again.
> What has? – Eternity.
> It is the sea, gone off
> With the sun.

"Nobody's topped that," she said entirely amused and turning back to him.

Page didn't turn, but into the mirror said, "I know, nobody."

Addie had black hair that fell in straw-like reeds, and a lightly freckled cheek on already yellowed skin. Her lips moved with the looks she gave; looks that never fell far from the truth of her feelings – the low-down, godforsaken truth. The hair scarf she wore coupled with her almond eyes, almost made her look like a gypsy, and it'd be alright with her if someone thought she was. She was a pretty girl, but was not gorgeous.

"So how have you been? I didn't get to see you last night," Addie asked, shutting the book and standing up. "You look a bit run down."

"Oh, well I sort of had a long day," Page said sitting on his bed, staring down as he untied his bootlaces.

Addie climbed behind him on the bed and draped her arms around him. "What did you do all day?" she asked, playfully biting into the bottom skin of his ear.

Page winced at her bite. "Not much really." In his head, he ran through the day and thought of something to pull from it. "I wrote a little –"

"Oh, what'd you write?" She interrupted.

"Just your note."

"Oh."

"Then I had a couple conversations with some people. Longwell and Colander stopped by, we talked. I didn't really do anything."

"Well do you want to go out and have a drink maybe? It's not very late."

"A drink?" Page asked looking down at his open shoelaces. "A drink would be nice."

The note Page wrote Addie was composed in the Diner Booth, a 24-hour joint on Huntington Street. Page was sitting next to the storefront window and

Addie's car was parked right outside, just on the other side of the sidewalk and the parking meters. Ketchup stains were on the table, and the salt was spilled over. The waitress dealt herself Solitaire at a table nearby. On stiff paper, Page quickly scribbled these lines:

Did it get mixed too hard? Too quickly? It's hard to tell in the sun if it's really rough. I can't find you. But I think I know where you may be. I've looked for you under the car and behind a beggar's shed. The engine backfired, and I came rolling out from underneath. The beggar played hardball, but he finally did tell me that you'd crossed the street with a chicken. He couldn't say why but he suggested I stay, and discuss the matter with him as a whole. The wind picked up down the alley, so I thought it best to decline, pick up my shoes, and ride after you. The beggar, becoming quite perturbed, waved a hand at my face as a distract, and smacked me in the forehead with a legal dose. He called me a jerk and pushed me out the door. I started going, but never found nothing showing. No shapes I'd not seen. No sounds I'd not heard. I said "look at that, there goes a bird. I think." I'm searching down street wells, water pipes, and in drain buckets for you. Come out cold and wet, with a serene drip running down my neck. I'm in the Diner Booth at 3:40 in the morning drying out, eating salted potato skins. I don't know what keeps me coming for you. It's somewhere down and just out of reach. But who cares? And why go finding it? It'll come back when you're with me and the sun too.

-Page

A mob boss ran Huntington Street. Hidden behind a blank expression on his walks, he gathered impressions or just got a couple names. On one of the street's corners two girls looked at each other, puffed their cigarettes at the same time, nodded, and crossed the road together. High boots and bug sunglasses. The look was hidden under dark shades or a long veil. A glance could be at anything. Street signs or the people crossing the white dotted line, coming from wherever it was they used to be. Nobody cared. A man moved here, a vagabond there. Rolling stones ran down the street, somebody had kicked them, and where they stopped and if they ever did nobody could know. If you weren't getting drunk, people smelt you like a skunk. Sniffing into trash bags, squirting at what may scare you. You were dead in the water. Better marry a rich man's daughter. A girl you'll find on Huntington Street named Rachel will sweet-talk into your ear until her voice is gone, you start to blush, but she's already left you. Paddle a rowboat across the Atlantic to have her do that again. Meg's never got anybody at the helm of the ship, but in the hold she's got two whiskies and a shoe-horn. Amanda, and you better not let your eyes slip down her. She'd have you by the waist and with a sweat coming down your face. Any Mary Anne you find there, you'll take in a second. She keeps the sun trapped in her hair and the honky-tonk in her boots. Speak to her about confessing, and she'll put a finger in your nose, plug you up.

A store's backroom was a place of business on Huntington Street. Inside them meetings carried out in haste dealt the cards, made the deals, and ran the street's show. The mob's show. Huntington Street was strictly under the control of the men willing to break joints, steal then move, and ready to go to any end to please the customer so long as a profit turned – and the proprietor wasn't the one getting caught. You could pretty much get anything you wanted for the price. Always, two men of theirs were there for one of yours, and on occasion someone who'd walked into the room was dragged out – sometimes kicking, sometimes not. Longwell and Colander sat anxiously in one such room on the same Saturday they'd been with Page. Now it was night.

Men dressed to the "T" in inconspicuty lined the bluest shade of red walls, and were engaged in the most general of chitchats. It was all part of the cover when anyone from the outside was around. The room was particularly small and bare. The paint on the wall being its boldest decoration. An undersized table with a few chairs was all that fit in the room as far as furniture. Three were on one side of the table, one on the other. A weak lamp sat on the table's edge and lit the room's lower half. Colander and Longwell had been brought there to receive details on the job they'd been offered, and it'd been expected that Page would be present too.

If there hadn't been a guy at the door, nobody would have heard the knock. It was once and thin. In the hallway waiting was a man once called Cortez – the man responsible for running Huntington Street's mob scene. Because of his business, he preferred to keep his current name to himself. This was of course for his own protection. Only a few knew it, and their lips were pinched tightly between his slender fingers.

The door was opened and then shut just after the man once called Cortez had entered. His hair was long, and his curls spirals. They hung out from under a white Panama hat and swayed along with his walk. His hat's brim was flimsy, but could be bent into place. It rimmed his forehead to keep the sun out. A skinny red feather stuck in the piece of ribbon running around the hat, and it bowed along its suede top. His black leather jacket was open, the leather stretched and broken-in though still dark and shiny. He sat in the lone chair that was across the table from the two younger men, and he did so without saying a word in voice or expression. The bottom of his chin to the tip of his nose was all that was in the light. Longwell could see facial hair, patches going up the man's jawbone and cheek, covering and curly in some spots, bare in others.

His white shirt was unbuttoned at the top and printed with blue dots. When Longwell took in the man's presence, he scrunched his face but thought better of saying anything. Colander just stared. The man talked slow, deliberate, and didn't really negotiate.

"Where's the other guy?" he asked.

The chair next to Colander and Longwell was empty.

"Not here," Longwell replied. "Couldn't make it tonight, but he's in. He'll be there."

The man nodded, but was displeased. "You're sure he's in? We need him. They may have three."

"Yeah, he's in," Longwell assured.

Colander's eyes moved back and forth across the table, from his friend to Cortez and around again to his friend. His knees kept moving, and he tried to get a look of the faces on the men standing around the room, but the light wasn't strong enough to see anything, there were only mid-sections and occasional smoke crossing into the light. Their conversations had dropped-off since the boss came in.

"The deal is a simple hand-off. One party handing the other the goods. Very simple. Because of that, you're asking for too much money," the boss told them. "That much is just not there for us to give you."

"Well, I thought those were the terms of the deal. That's what the guy told me. That's what we had agreed upon." Longwell countered.

"Agreed upon? Kid, what do you take me for? This is no agreement. Nothing has happened. Agreements leave trails. Get us all in trouble. We have an understanding. Now we both understand that if the hand-off goes through without a hitch, then there will be financial retribution that finds you. I'm sorry if you had assumed that amount of money would be what found you. No longer the case. Now I don't know you, you don't know me. You see me coming down the street, you walk right past as if I'm the ugliest bitch you've ever seen. Ya got it?" His voice never rose, but his attention was caught.

Colander swallowed hard and his knees sped up. He looked to Longwell who tried his best to keep his face straight and not give anything away.

"Huh? Am I ugly?" He pushed forward the hook of his nose, though they still could not see the whole of his face.

Colander answered, "You're ugly".

Everyone in the room looked at him.

Cortez turned back to Longwell. His chair creaked as he pushed against its back. Though the two friends couldn't see it, the man's eyes just barely could stay open. The looks he gave were hid by the hat's brim and the room's darkness. But once one could see his whole face, it was clear to categorize his expressions as dried up and sullen. Though first and foremost, one would find it impossible to miss the feminine qualities that strained his face. He almost always looked as if he were pleading, but his voice he didn't let match. His eyes betrayed the business. They made him seem soft, vulnerable, eased into his melancholy. It was true that in his closest circle, he often did express his desire to just go home. Back to the farm he was said to have somewhere outside the city. Home where his wife waited, pale brown skinned and olive eyed. Freckle nosed and coaled black hair. She kept the farm running while he was away, though she spent the sunrise painting landscapes.

"Deal's in two weeks. Two," the man put up his fingers. "We'll see what we have to pay you. You'll get what it's worth."

Longwell stood up from the chair and headed out the door without saying a word – the inconspicuous men politely obliging a path. Colander followed. The man once named Cortez turned to watch the door shut, and then looked back down at the table.

"That, 'Huh? Am I ugly?' bit," he said to his men, only turning to them by the neck. "I thought of it on the way over," he explained facing forward again. "Thought it would sound good." He scraped his finger across the table top, looked at what had collected on its tip, and then got up.

"It was good, boss."

Cortez questioned that with a shrug and a glum smile.

Colander walked through the night alone. His apartment was one of the last on Huntington's west end. The wind sent a sheet of the newspaper across the street. Colander watched as it toppled end-over-end, careening loosely, flimsily, and only in motion until the wind had it not be. In his periphery, he noticed a figure's shadow moving across the wall of the building ahead of him. A dog barked from four buildings behind. Colander quickened his pace and soon was only a few houses away from his own. On the building ahead of him, the bobbing shadow reappeared, flattened in the alleyway, and then popped up on the next building's side. By the time he reached his door, Colander was nearly running a sprint – his long legs striding him along. Half-way up the stairs, he froze and scanned the street to spot his follower. He saw nothing and was turning back towards the door to put in his key, when the shadow appeared on the wall of the building just past his. He inspected the sidewalk, but the streetlight's glare and night's darkness are excellent covers for those who wish to haunt in them, and Colander could see nothing.

The three friends were sitting at the Fish Kettle the next day, outside still. The day was sunny, and a steady breeze kept the street smell moving, so nobody dwelled on the reek of piss or spilt wine. A man at the table next to them told everyone he was twenty-two, but he looked more like thirty-five. Dressed in a suave black suit with leather boots and a light blue undershirt, his face was a foot long, and his receding hairline went back nearly one too. Johnny, he said was his name, and his hair went straight and long just like his legs. He was up past six-foot-three like a toothpick. Upon leaving for the Fish Kettle that afternoon, he had estimated the number of women he presumed could be there on this, one of the fall's very last, perfectly weathered days. On his way he stopped at a peddling vendor's cart and bought the amount of roses equal to his woman estimate. Longwell glared at Johnny as he handed each lady there her rose. Striding table to table. They'd sniff the petals and giggle. The Portuguese waiter was tan and moved in blue-jean overalls. He brought out drinks.

"The guy told me $50,000," Longwell explained.

"Well I'd say at the meeting, the boss seemed a little put-off by that figure," Colander deduced.

"No shit," Longwell replied. "And did you see those other guys too? They'd be scraping our guts off the wall for weeks if we put up a fight. That or they'd just throw us out on our broke ass. Anyways, we can do this. We'll be getting some money. Easy money, baby. No big deal," Longwell was excited and looked around the table, first to Page then to Colander.

"You are doing 'babies' now?" Page noticed from behind the lip of his coffee mug.

"What?" Longwell asked, not as if he didn't hear, but as if to wonder why Page would question the catch-phrase.

"Longwell, you don't know what the hell you're doing. I certainly don't either."

Colander quietly decided if he knew what to do.

"What is there to know? You hand somebody something, and they hand you back something else. Am I missing a step here? Plus, a fucking guy could roll a cannon down this street, have a machete in his coat pocket, and nobody would even look twice. The beauty is – nobody does it."

"You know, I'm glad I didn't go to that meeting. I don't want some fucking mob guy getting a look of my face, thinking about me, being able to recognize me, or uhhh –"

"Mob guy? It's barely the mob. It's not the

Mafia. Just a couple entrepreneurs like us here, trying to make a buck. And we're doing the smallest, tiniest, job for them. A simple hand-off. It's not something to worry about. Sil's not sitting around in the backroom of the Bada-Bing waiting for you. He's got his do-rag back on, he's hanging with Springsteen again. Anyways, you didn't go cause you're a little schoolboy bitch," Longwell concluded.

Colander laughed. Strangely enough, his laugh was exceptionally loud. It always was, he had no soft laugh, it was loud or nothing. A frugal word-user, a greedy laugher.

"When you get that sand outta your vagina why don't you come on back, then we'll sit down like men, have our little talk," Longwell was straight faced and waved his hand back towards himself as he spoke.

The waiter stood over the suave Johnny, and took orders from his two new high-heeled friends. The English of the waiter was perfect, his accent British.

"That fucking guy," Longwell said. "Who does he think he is in that suit?"

Colander looked over towards Johnny smugly, and then stared with a blank face at the table in front of him. Page looked down the street.

"I think somebody was following me last night," Colander announced quietly.

The other two eyed him for a moment.

"You know, you're right, Page. I don't know what I'm doing," Longwell said taking a sip of his drink.

"Just like I didn't the time we were pushing Tony." He adjusted the ice cubes in his mouth.

"Pushing it? Oh, yeah. That took a lotta pushing. Besides, this is nothing like that."

"Come on, we were making those parties every night," Longwell said.

"Yeah, then breaking them too," Colander finished, and they all laughed.

Page began a story. "This girl comes up to Colander, she gets on her tipy-toes and starts giving him these little peck kisses on the lips cause he's getting her more fucked up than she ever has been before,"

"Ha! That was crazy. I was thinking, 'uhh, what am I supposed to do here?'"

"Yeah, right. You knew what you were doing. You kissed her back. Meanwhile, some kid's freaking out on in the bathroom, pouring water all over himself and more pleading that he's gonna be alright than convincing us. Slark and Cristi stay on the couch all night following lines with a bump. Molly's totally jazzed up. She keeps telling me the same fucking story every hour, won't shut up, and I can't keep my legs still nor stop staring at her tits – I love the girl. But yeah, I'd say you broke the party right up the ass." Page turned his palms up and had a breath of laughter. He took a sip of the coffee and scratched the back of his neck.

Colander laughed, while Longwell fondly shook his head to the memory and picked up his drink. Page looked past them and to the suave suit man's table.

Johnny whispered into the ear of one girl and had his hand on the leg of the other.

Page took another sip of coffee, set it down carefully on the table, and puckered his lips to its bitterness. He traced his finger along the handle of the teaspoon sitting in the saucer. He'd yet to shave that day, and a haircut was probably in need as his hair had become more and more bushy. He was trying to think, but there was only void, a hole, a gap in his mind that he was unable to step over. "Alright, let's do it. I'm in." He flicked his middle and pointer finger against the tabletop repeatedly. "Fuck it."

Twelve days prior to that agreement, nearly three hours past noon, Longwell was coming out of the Fish Kettle. He came out alone and headed straight for the side-alley that split the bar and a local junk shop, Harold's Store of All Things. Longwell smacked his hand against Harold's, leaned against the store's wall and pissed on it. He yawned and tried shaking his head clear. Once he was halfway back to the sidewalk, another man turned down the alley. Longwell kept walking towards him as he'd yet to notice. His shoulders were almost as wide as the alleyway, and the uneven pavement tipped him side-to-side, running his shoulders into both buildings. The approaching man was of no particular description. He put an arm around Longwell as if they knew each other, and Longwell couldn't remember if they did. The man spoke in a clear tone and delivered the speech at a volume audible only to its sole audience member, though nobody else was around to overhear anyways.

"Good money?" Longwell responded, drunk. He said calmly, "Hell yeah".

The man whispered into his ear again.

"That is good money."

The man nodded.

After agreeing upon going through with the deal, the three friends left the Fish Kettle and walked down Huntington Street without speaking. They passed through a group of students and Longwell, forced to relinquish the sidewalk on account of the group, stepped gingerly into the road.

"Nietzsche man, Nietzsche," one of the students called for. "Through his words is how we should be considering this. 'Prudence', he wrote, 'created law in order to put an end to feuding, to useless squandering between forces of similar strength. But just as definitive an end will come if one party becomes decisively weaker than the other.'"

"Awwww, yeah! Cliff, man! Yes," Cliff's friend raised his hand in the air for a five up high. Cliff jumped to slap it and upon coming back down, he had to readjust his black brick seeing glasses, as they'd nearly fallen off his face.

"What the fuck's with those kids?" Longwell asked looking back at them.

"I don't know, Longwell," Colander answered quietly.

"It's like every single person here thinks they're so goddamn cool because they've read a fucking book.

Going around reciting lines from it as if there's some prize for being the biggest douchebag on the block."

"You think that's what it is?"

"Yes Colander, I do," Longwell said as if answering labored him.

The conversation paused.

"Alright, so two relief pitchers are sitting in the bullpen next to each other," Longwell began a joke. "One of them says to the other, 'Fuck man'," Longwell jumped smoothly back onto the sidewalk. "'Manager hasn't called my number in a goddamned six games.' 'Six games?' the other guy says back surprised. 'Yeah. Some shit's going on. I know it.' He looks seriously over at the other pitcher and he says, 'I think my wife's giving everyone in the dugout blowjobs while I sit out here. Manager won't put me in so I don't find out.' 'Oh yeah?' the other guy says back. 'What makes you think that?' 'Well,' the guys says, 'I know she likes to suck the balls, and that shit's gotta be able to secrete outta the skin or something. Plus I've noticed she's bulked up, her head's shrunk, and the bitch has hit like ten dingers in her last eight town-softball games.'"

A van turned down Huntington Street on its west end. The one-way street had two ends, east and west. The west an entrance and the east an exit. The end portions of the street ran perpendicular to the two subsidiary roads. Two corners made up the street's middle third, creating a ninety-degree turn, and joining the other thirds, which were in the shape of L's – one "L" upside down and the other backwards. The middle portion of the street ran parallel to the two subsidiaries. The approaching van clumsily took the ninety-degree turn, the ride becoming parallel to Huntington's feeder roads, and the vehicle began to crawl real slowly, and before the second bend it eased into its parking space, the engine killed.

The origin of the street's name is a bit too deeply buried to dig-up. There are far too many worthy Huntington's in the world to pin anything particular to its namesake. The Order of Skull and Bones, a secret gentlemen's society at one point known as The Brotherhood of Death, had a co-founder with the middle name Huntington. There is Huntington's Disease as well. Rare and hereditary, it manifests in the brain at middle age and leaves one with the twitches, disturbing their speech, and kicking them down into fits of dementia. Now these would be silly things to name a street after, but who knows, there are a lot of silly things out there.

The street had become somewhat of a hamlet. A villa. There was an influx from the world outside, but if one were so inclined, they may easily choose to stay tucked in for awhile and never once leave the home that harbored them. Plenty did. Life existed in other places too. Somewhere else citizens moved around, bumped into one another and pled their case. But Huntington Street's lights came on at night, its sidewalks were as clean as any other street's. Its sewers flowed. Individual brick made up the road itself, each dulled from red, some stuck at the bottom of puddles, some missing all together.

A reason to go someplace else cropped up now and then, but amid those life pockets, most of the street's residents let their toenails grow against Huntington's sidewalk cement. The use of bricks on the street continued and piled up into enough buildings to keep a village's worth of people. And these people lived on top of the second-hand clothes boutiques and the cafes, 24-hour restaurants, and the bars keeping racks of burgundy, vodka, and wine for drowning. Five to six floors of apartments rose above the businesses, and on the rooftops too people congregated to feel more alive and kill their lifetime.

There was a Lady of Huntington Street. Young golden skinned and green eyed. At the street's west end, she lived in a white Victorian mansion. Days she spent leaning on her elbows, peering down bored onto the street-passers from her second-story veranda. An iron fence ran the length of the porch and created the illusion of her being caged in. When she slept, the night was under a silken blanket, completely still. But most nights there was no sleep. Tangled in the sheets and huffing on lovers' shoulders, they rested while watching the moon get shined out. Shipped in from the outside, The Lady of Huntington Street collected, used, and quickly discarded these muscle-chested men. Not always broad, but she preferred men who ate chicken instead of beef and whose arms, be them thin or thick, could wrap around what she was about. She wanted back door men. Men, not a man. The devil may be a woman.

The four men stepped from the van's back slider-door and two got out the front. They stretched and yawned while getting their feet back on the ground. One of them was much older than the others. The elder placed a hat on his head after shutting the passenger door. His black Urban Sombrero matched his black suit, and the cream sheepskin boots tied up to right below the knees would bring anyone's attention to him. The other five made up the members of the band – Marshmallow Overcoat.

If called upon, the bassist could do a twiddle on the fiddle too. Strain in his face and coming out the words he sung, bass notes slapped in-between. The guitarist had a Jew father and a Mohawk mother. His navy blue blazer was unbuttoned and subtle white stripes ran thinly down it. A scarf hung from his neck, which he usually kept untied. He'd hit the same lick four times in a row just to make sure it'd spike. Swinging the guitar from his thin frame with the pick raised, juicing it. A Southern redhead hit the drums. Taught down in Arkansas to talk out a toneless drawl, he cooked there in a Rock 'n' Roll melting pot and sung like a Southerner too. Two piano players were in the band, and one of them was its tallest member. They both had full beards. The tall one had a goofy smile, the other did not smile.

The band played mythology and put it out in traditional blues that could move. They sung tall-tale epics – riddling looming figures, crying for those buried in their own wallow, and tunes that turned loose women and booze into the refugee's sanctuary. All folk. It was by late morning that they arrived on Huntington Street. They'd played a show the night before somewhere else, and tribulations from years on the road had inclined them to fall to their knees and kiss the ground of each town they left. They came in with a fog attached and hid from the day in the Fish Kettle, the not-so clean, not-so refined, drinking house Page, Longwell, Colander, and their friends frequented. Marshmallow Overcoat would be playing there that night.

When the six of them walked in, the maitre d' cleaned a table and pretended not to notice their raggedness – though it wouldn't have kept them from being served anyways. Inside, the six of them could wait the sun out.

The only people who went into the Fish Kettle were regulars or people who did not know anything about the place. Regulars carelessly flicked its door open and wouldn't be able to help a giggle as they entered, really with just the slightest bit of embarrassment, nothing they'd couple real feelings to. The slacks wearing family-man walked in and wouldn't put a second foot down before picking his child up, holding the kid close to his chest, and rushing the way out before the door could close. In light of this phenomenon, only a certain crowd was ever in there. No mixed company.

Inside, a patron may shout: "We listen to Phish! Not ahhh…not ahhh, Tchaikovsky or some old-timer for it! He was their guy, we have ours. It's a damn shame those bastard hippies had to come ruin Phish. Spread their peace, love, and, ahhh, patchouli. I'll drown their fucking head in a puddle of patchouli! Peace and love? I don't think so – Phish harnessed chaos. You want peace and love? Head back to your commune, hippie. This ain't no place for that," and he would down his drink. Or another conversation may go: "Did you see the Planet Earth when the bats were falling off the ceiling and being suffocated in a pile of their own shit? I mean, shit man, in your own shit? Does that not define the irony of living?" he continued before anyone could respond, "I can't remember which episode it was in – Caves – nobody can ever remember what episode things happened in for that show, everyone gets fucked up for it, you know?" he waited for the silence after everyone's laughter. "To appreciate the mind-shattering of it, to its fullest, most can't be in any regular state-of-mind. I can't." Other sorts of conversations took place too.

The current day went by like an ocean tide. In came the waitress, slow creeping at first and not coming too often, just carrying a drink every now and then. Coffee and teas, or whatever else they asked for. Not many people were there, and conversations waned and waxed, none of them lasting too long, neither digging too deep nor liable to last much more than a couple exchanges. Each band member catching his breath.

"Yeah, so what's your sign?" The piano player who did smile asked a woman he'd just met.

"Ummm, Gemini?"

"Ahhh, a two-sided queen, I see now. Hmmm," he put an interested finger to his mouth and nodded in understanding.

She laughed and sipped her drink.

"Honey tell me, you seem in-tune with the world around you, do you ever think we're put here just to float around oblivious to everything going on? Not on any search for reason, answers, or truth? Just here for the scenery, you know?" The piano man elaborated with his hands as he spoke.

"Well," she thought.

"I don't know about you, but I've found that anything I know, once it's turned on its head or given just the slightest push of breath out my mouth, will appear without question, without a doubt, flat and deadly wrong. Like it just doesn't then make the slightest sense. It puts me down to crawling. Desolate and afraid of anything – counting on the revelation I know won't come to raise me to my feet again," he finished staring into his scrambled eggs.

"I do think that sometimes!" She yelled out.

He looked up and gave a wide grin before laughing himself away.

A painting by a Picasso imitator had been stolen by a ruffian patron, and hung now off a nail in the Fish Kettle's wall. The band's guitarist had spotted the painting from across the room and now took long steps towards it. Its young man wore a dark overcoat and from beneath it his white shirt puffed out at the neck. A rip from Picasso's blue period. His skin color was sickly cream, and his face misaligned into a bored stare at the wine glass in front of him. Observers often wondered what he could be thinking about so pensively and with such gloom. The guitarist was hardly worried about something so obvious. He pressed his thumb onto the corner of the painting's frame. Rubbing to feel the wood grains.

"This one's something," he said into a cigarette.

Page opened his door without the key. He hardly ever locked it. As he came inside, he was informed, though not surprised, that he had unexpected visitors.

"Where'd you go? Double D Addie's?" Longwell asked.

"She doesn't have double D's. She doesn't have big tits at all."

"Hey, take it easy. It's a fucking joke," Longwell paused. "By the way, will you fucking leave this girl already? She's yesterday's news, and a self-righteous bitch at that. I don't know how you're so infatuated with her."

"What the fuck did you just say?"

"What?"

"Can you not say things like that about her please? You don't know what you're even talking about," Page dismissed. "She's a bitch to you because you – sometimes I think purposefully – will do anything just to rile her up," Page said while scratching a finger deep into his eye to itch it.

"Me? She always starts it. I'm sorry, once she comes at me with that bullshit, I'm gonna let her have it," Longwell said plainly. "You don't see it happen.

You're the one oblivious to anything ever going on."

"Oblivious? Alright Longwell, enlighten me. Tell me about everything that's going on."

Colander turned his attention from the TV to watch the rising conversation.

"Enlighten you? Yeah, right. You're like trying to screw a thousand watt light bulb into a sixty. It won't work, and the house might blow up if it does. "

Colander opened his mouth, "She does have nice tits. Nice, not big, but nice."

"I know," Page coldly agreed. He dropped his keys on the living room table, and walked into the kitchen.

The apartment Page lived out of was organized into a mess. The living room's TV was small and tucked in the corner of the room with all the seats facing it. Scattered on green walls, obscure and familiar hangings of photos and paintings, some hand cropped, others as found, hung out for display. There was a bedroom, a bathroom off it, and a kitchen that the apartment opened up to. The living room had the TV setup as well as a chair and desk, and there was a coat closet, but most coats got tossed over the furniture for their hanging.

Page sat on the couch and rested his head against the hard wall. The couch's back cushion didn't extend higher than his neck despite his being particularly slight. The couch was slighter. Only one person could comfortably fit on it. A rectangular coffee table made of wood filled the room proportionately, Longwell had his feet up on it, and he sat in the room's best seat, a leather recliner. Misplaced ash strewed between two trays, and some had made it only to the tops of yesterday's still-out newspaper. Longwell held the TV's remote and constantly switched the channels. During the show, he chewed the remote's end.

"Will you sit like a normal person?" Longwell said.

"I'm comfortable," Page replied.

Longwell turned back to the TV. Colander sat in a chair that had no legs, sitting flat on the ground opposite the leather chair, between them was the coffee table.

"Oh, I forgot the game was on," Longwell said. He moved too fast down the channels and the football game flicked on for a second and then was gone.

"God – damn it."

He was right back on the game.

"Great, fucking John Madden. The old crone." Page said bothered and adjusted himself on the couch. His butt had fallen asleep.

"Come on. Don't you want to hear about playing in leather helmets? How they need to play some 'smash-mouth football'? Football. Not golf? Why fucking do they have to say football there?"

"It just means they need to play tougher," Colander explained.

"I – know – what – it means."

"Well?" Colander put his hands up.

"Forget it," but then Longwell didn't. "It's a matter of redundancy."

"You're getting to be a little redundant yourself," Colander said and turned back to the football game.

They sat in a silence lasting three plays.

"Hey man, I'm sorry about before, I shouldn't have said that about Addie." Longwell apologized. "*I just get so crazy sometimes, baby,*" he spoke tenderly.

"Get outta here, don't use your boyfriend voice with me," Page said trying not to laugh. "Don't worry about it. I know where your heart is."

"Yeah," Longwell nodded.

Tom Brady threw a five yard pass that turned into ten, and the commentators lavished him with praise, the cameraman zoomed into his facemask.

"There they go again, as if Tom Brady is the re-incarnation of Christ," Longwell chewed on the end of the remote. "They all suck his dick."

"Why don't you stop sucking the remote's dick? What's wrong with you?" Page said raising his voice. "I gotta use that."

Longwell took the remote out of his mouth without looking away from the TV.

Page cupped his hands over his eyes, though he kept both open. The darkness did wonders for them, and with no sight, no glimpse, nor light to try – his eyes eased into the peace of nothing.

"I'd follow Tom Brady right off the cliff,"

Colander declared. "That's just the kinda leader he is."

Page said nothing.

The game went to commercial for its first quarter's end, but John Madden came back on the television screen. There was a brand new way to loose your athlete's foot, and John was there to tell everyone about it. Longwell's impression had a crack in it which made his voice sound more like commentary from the '94 video game than true to real life, but still the other two laughed when he said, "Not only does Tom Brady have one of the best arms in football, but he's hung like a Clydesdale too."

Page kept his hands over his face as he laughed behind them.

A couple dressed up in royal blue soldier suits walked the street hot in the middle of a debate. They were east of Page's apartment, though soon to be walking by it. The woman disputed the man deceptively, and their partnership in an upcoming doubles chess tournament, for which they'd previously enrolled in, seemed as though it may be in jeopardy. The tournament was not to be held on Huntington Street. The pair took their walks across the entire city. They were cutting through Huntington. For miles, they would discuss anything and all of it. Today it was plans of attack, strategy, and chess.

"No, you're wrong. I won't let you throw the pawn in, it's too bold an opening move." The man made a fist.

"What do you mean? If we don't attack now, how's that going to look? You have to throw the pawn in."

"We can creep them forward, strategically and with the proper backing, but we can't dump a wheelbarrow full of 'em into the fire!"

"You and your theatrical metaphors. Always such the drama queen. If it's not a fire, it's the coming of another Ice Age."

"Another Ice Age is coming! Polar bears, soon you'll see 'em – walking around – ahhh – in California even! Of course, that is if they can swim," he paused for a moment. "But I don't know what you're talking about. I'm no queen," he resignedly turned his head away from her.

"Look, we tell them whatever we want. It doesn't make much a difference. There's a reason they only go forward – suit 'em up, kick 'em in the butt. Dump them, whatever. If we wanted an opinion on the matter, we need go no further than to stick our heads out the window and catch some common's utterance in the passing wind. No we don't need a tongue, just a pair of feet for the boots."

The man looked back to his wife. "I don't think I like what you're saying."

A young resident on his bicycle whizzed down the street, his coat tails caught up in the wind. The three friends came out of Page's apartment just as he rode by. They were by now properly prepared to go to the Fish Kettle and see the Marshmallow Overcoat show. Longwell stood on the sidewalk's edge, a step from the street, while Page jiggled his key to get it out of the lock. Colander was just out the doorway with his feet spread wide in a stance, hands in his pockets, whistling to himself. The width of the sidewalk separated Longwell from the other two. The bike rider steered his course right through the gap and stuck his tongue out in a funny face at Page and Colander, making a strange cat-call as he zoomed by. To avoid the bicycler, Longwell more likely fell off the sidewalk than he did step down it.

"Woop-woop," Colander called back after the rider had whizzed by.

"Oh, what? You think you're so badass on your bike?" Longwell yelled and got tough, but couldn't keep from smiling. He turned to find his friends. "Hey, seems the real badasses wear corduroy sports coats now, and have long faggy hair. See?" he pointed and stumbled.

Page smiled and put an arm around his friend. Longwell's shoulders had to be wide to top his round midsection, so Page's arm just barely could make it across.

"Come here, you big lug."

"What? What?" Longwell laughed.

They crossed the street together and came up a few steps behind the soldier couple.

"Look at these fuckers," Page pointed at the soldiers. He left his friends, caught up to the couple and started marching, as if in perfect regiment, behind them. Stiff and shoulders hunched. His arms swung like the Terminator would run, and Colander from behind, counted out, "1, 2, 3, 4".

The couple had yet to notice him, and their debate continued.

"A bishop? You want to throw the bishop in there now too? Have you no end, woman?"

Page marched in straight-faced, real authoritative-like and now with a hand on his brow, all much to the surprise of the soldiers.

"Yes, sir! General, sir! Reporting for the duty of being shipped to the crumbling frontlines of Anytown, Planet Earth, sir!" Page's eyes were somewhere above the male soldier's head, and his words barked. His voice softened, "Please, take me. I have nothing left, nothing else but to go fire off my gun, try to kill anybody I can." His character broke, and he looked the woman in the eye, "Oh, ma'm. My deepest apologies. I didn't notice you were the one wearing the pants."

"The pants?" inquired the male.

Colander and Longwell had stopped just behind, and the two watched with half interest.

"I'm wearing pants," the male soldier smugly remarked.

"Deepest apologies, ma'm!" Page was back into the charade, one arm in tight to his body and the other bringing his hand back to the brow. "But, your permission to speak freely, honestly, sincerely, speculatively, informatively, without a single straight face? And," he acted the pause, "just a hair under the drink too."

The man said nothing, just stared, and the woman's honor could only let her gawk on the inside.

"Have you performed your Adolf Eichmannian duties today?" Page asked.

"Our what?" The woman became even more

agitated, and though she didn't know who Adolf Eichmann was, she fell immediately into offense at the inclusion of her with any name so German it could only belong to a Nazi.

"So what do you think it really says about you if you're Hitler's best henchman? Most loyal attendant? And always his right-hand man? Hey, he's the Fuhrer, top dog, not bad, right?" Page wagged his elbow.

"You absurd child! Going around all drunk with your friends. Get out of here. Take your delusions with you. Learn some manners why don't you. I don't know what bag you've been sniffing in, but go get some respect for yourself and for the soldiers who make possible the very freedoms you flaunt."

Colander and Longwell roared into laughter at the site of this woman giving it to their friend. As the woman's voice rose, they couldn't help but pay more attention.

"You think your bottle will keep you free? Will protect you? Save you from yourself?" she continued.

"Power to the bottle, baby!" Longwell shouted, raising his hands.

"Well, write your note, roll it into the bottle, and flush your S.O.S. down the toilet. Someone then should surely save you," she smiled and Page said nothing. "Now that I think about it though, please do join up, we could use somebody like you – on the frontline."

"I have no idea what either of you two are

talking about," the male soldier shook his head and stopped listening.

"Make possible the freedoms I flaunt? No soldier out waving around his gun in god knows what country is making me free. It's the citizens, their refusal to be denied anything, they are the ones who protect me. Gunpoint is no place for freedom."

"You see the little picture, my boy. Just an idealistic, merry, little picture. You know what peace does? It reassures those Adolf Eichmannians you speak of that if they pick up a gun and shoot you in the head, then there's nobody there to stop them. It's easy to shoot some bumbling drunk in the head. Isn't it?" she asked her male companion.

"A shot? Oh, no thank you. Ever since I woke up that morning covered in marker drawings, head-to-toe, obscenities and ummm, well, anatomical drawings, since then, well no, no more shots for me," he said chuckling. "We have the chess tournament anyways, remember? Geeze. Drunk chess. That's funny."

Page turned back to the woman, "I guess we'll have to agree to disagree then."

"See you in hell," she ended.

The Fish Kettle's houselights went dark. A spotlight popped and fell onto a lone microphone. Wearing the same black Urban Sombrero over his suit and the sheepskin boots on his feet, the old gentleman walked nonchalantly from offstage and came into the light. He stepped to the microphone, cleared his throat. He recited these lines as if he knew just what to say:

The River God's story finished. He fell silent. The whole company stirred in the miracle he'd related; all except Ixion's son, who laughed at them for believing such a tale. Arrogant and contemptuous of the gods as he was, to his host he challenged. 'Your story, it is of pure invention, Aeschylus,' he said. 'Far too much faith you put in the power of the gods if you think they can give and take the shapes of things,' he said. All those around fell dumbfounded, shook their heads, disapproving of such words. Before any other could speak, Lelex, ripe in years and wisdom, came forward. Finger raised, he proclaimed:

"The power of heaven is measureless mere son, knows not the bounds of Earth, sun, or moon, and it pushes down in vengeance on those who speak otherwise.

Believe me or not, it will not matter. But here, I will tell you a story to prove it."

The old gentleman ran a hand through the end of his beard. He had hardly even acknowledged the audience. A lackadaisical turn, and he was out of the spotlight and moving in an even walk. Once he was off, the light disappeared.

"Good evenin'," a Southerner's voice said from the dark.

After the show, the friends split up for the night. Addie had come too. She and Page went to his apartment. Like many, Colander and Longwell stayed at the Fish Kettle for the rest of the night, and spent the dark putting the day's light behind them. Page's apartment was only a couple buildings away, so before the bartender could even fulfill the crowd with another round, Page and Addie had begun to climb into bed.

"Do you think the look a musician gives when he's performing is for the note he's hitting, is just about to hit, or just has?" Page asked tripping over his jeans as he kicked them off.

"You think he would always know the note he's about to play?" Addie asked.

"He must know it somewhere. Otherwise why else would he hit that particular one?"

"It has to be the one he just hit."

"Why?" Page challenged.

"Because."

"How do you know the body can compute two separate actions so quickly?"

Addie gave the look of a child disapproving. The look sharply questioned, almost facetiously criticized, but had the feminine cuteness to cover it. And had it not been for its common occurrence and his numbing, Page would have stopped her right there to kiss her for it. She could always be cute.

As he climbed into bed he said, "The fingers are far from the face, and even if a synapse can fire real fast, there still needs to be time for the note struck to travel out the guitar, through the cord, to the amp, go through the amp, into the ear, through the brain, and into the face. You mean to tell me all this can happen in, what we see, as an instant?"

"You have no idea what you're talking about."

"No idea? How is any of that wrong?" he asked sitting up and putting on a disbelieving smile.

"You're just dumb," she said in a little voice, while raising her shoulders. She got into bed next to him, and swept her hand through his hair.

"I am not dumb," he leaned into her hand.

"I like you dumb," she smiled back. "Besides, it's all a sham anyways. They make those faces just for show. It's got more to do with playing the part than playing the note."

"Fakers?"

"Yes."

"You a faker?"

"Yes. But my face is for the note you're just about to pluck," she said crawling on top of him and sticking her face in his. "I feel it coming."

"You lie," he said kissing her lip.

"No, I'm no liar." she said breaking away. "I

fake. You, you do too. I see you stumbling, bumbling, a ragamuffin, waddling down the street. Is that you?"

"I in no way – waddle."

"You think you walk cool."

"I don't need to think that."

"Oh," she mocked, and climbed off Page and then the bed. On the floor were his boots, his jeans, and hat. Dressed in her underwear and tank-top, she slipped her tiny feet into the boots and put the hat on.

"What are you doing?"

"I'm you," she replied. "You, Colander, and Longwell. Well Longwell – he waddles. But you all walk like this." She puckered her lips under his hat, let her shoulders fall down, and her hips slip into each step. She walked the length of his bedroom.

"I do not walk like that. And a ragamuffin? What the hell is that?"

"You're right, your face stays angrier," she said, fixing her look.

Page watched from the bed. After a moment's contemplation, he chose to stay quiet, and allow Addie to remain on.

She talked in his voice. "I choose to exile myself in anonymity. If I ever were to marry a woman, she'd have to be an invincible, hair low-hanging, insurmountable, *broad*," she said facing Page, leaning back as if she had her thumbs in belt-buckles. "A real *chick*. Make her my *woman*."

"I don't talk like that."

"I'll drink my beer," she continued with a clumsy step in the boots, "lap-up my wine," she took another step, "lady just show me a good time. You take one more of those, and you'll surely be mine," she came to a stop right at the foot of the bed, staring over Page.

"You're something else," he said laughing at her.

"Oh, thank you," she said bowing and removing the hat.

"Take those off – get over here."

On the next day, a breezy sun-filled day, Page and Addie left his apartment in the late morning. They passed other residents, some walking, some sitting with a drink and their paper, some were whistling. Each person moving along through their idle time. Addie's black zipper-up sweatshirt hood was tight over her head, and kept the day's wind from cutting through her. With hair covered, left out was only her face. Page walked a step in front as Addie bubbled behind him.

"Addie," he said. "What are you bubbling all around for?"

"Oh, I don't know," she nudged him. "It just feels like the kind of day to be happy. It's sunny out, see?" she asked taking his arm by the bicep and sniffing into the air.

"Yeah. It is," he looked up at the sun. "You know? You're right – why not today? Seems just as good as any other," Page affirmed happily.

She smiled up at him, delighted in her passing of the good mood. "So what do you want to do today? I was thinking we could take a train ride out to the ocean. Do you want to? The beach would be deserted this time of year, the sun warm. We could fly a kite in this wind! Can we fly a kite?" Her hands were now bunched in the sweatshirt's stomach pocket, and she continued to bubble.

"Yeah, let's go to the beach," Page agreed. He cupped a hand around her hooded head.

She looked back at him and smiled. "To the beach," she pointed forward. "Should we walk? Huh? You wanna walk?"

Page looked at her smiling and he slightly laughed.

Overhead two helicopters hovered loudly, though they remained fairly high. They circled around for a moment or two, and then stationed themselves directly over the street. Page looked at them with a concern that bordered paranoia.

"No, let's take the train," he said.

The man once referred to as Cortez headed south on the sidewalk, walking right towards them. He held an umbrella to block the sunlight. Having not attended the meeting, Page did not recognize him. The man's shirt-sleeve reached just a bit short on the arm holding his umbrella, exposing his locked wrist, its thinness and frailty seemed to be the beginning of malnourishment. The umbrella caught Page's attention, and he likened it to one an ancient Japanese emperor might carry around. So he thought. Its shield a tight paper parchment, tan colored, and stretched over thin wooden rods that extended an inch beyond the top and curved delicately into ornament. The umbrella was small, its shadow cast no further than the man's own head. But he held to it, blocked the sun, and hid in its shade. Page and Addie walked by, and the man eyed them both behind his sunglasses, his face bothered though it remained somewhat vacant.

A fall day at the beach is not spent in swimsuits. The sun that had sparked the beach venture had given way to clouds by the time the two reached the shore. Addie let out a hard breath, and disappointment fell over her face as they reached the beachfront. She looked up and made a whimper at Page who stood beside her. He shrugged his shoulders and started to walk towards the water anyways.

The clouds rolled in ominously, creeping and swirling, and in shades of grey that cast a shadow on the churning ocean waves. The waves came in a beat, crashed the dry land and then left – the low-tide keeping millions of beach rocks uncovered. Page led them through the sand, down to the up-rushing waves and amongst the rocks. Addie had her feet in the water for a little bit, but soon got too cold. Page sat, his pant-legs rolled midway up his calves, and he picked up stones and threw them back into the ocean.

"Those helicopters," he began. "Seemed like cops."

"Cops? Why would cops be circling Huntington Street?"

"I don't know," Page said and then remained

quiet for a moment. "Law enforcers, government people, they like to once and awhile kick up the rug and see what's been under it.

"I hate cops," Addie said turning to the ocean. "If I can drive my car under control, going no matter how fast, then what the hell do they need to pull me over for? Filling quotas, taking my hard earned money, and trying to make me feel like shit." She picked up a rock and threw it into the ocean. "That's all they do. I just keep on driving now, as if I already know, 'there are no cops on this road'," she said in a voice of serene, naïve, hope. "Eighty miles-an-hour, ninety," she looked over, smiled, "one-hundred. No cops."

Page laughed and threw another rock into the water.

"I just pretend they'll never be there," she said.

"Usually they're not." Page squinted his eyes and looked over the ocean's horizon.

A mutual silence passed, more clouds seemed to be coming in. The mother of a young family further down the beach gathered her children's toys and corralled them back to their beach blanket.

"Do you like being with me?" Addie asked, looking him eye-to-eye.

"Of course, Addie. What would make you say that?"

A wind shot in, and blew through the hair that stuck-out of her hood. She held tighter to his arm.

"I don't know. I just like hearing you say it, I

guess."

Page winced at her vulnerability. "I don't hang around people that I don't like," he told her. "Any morning I wake up next to you, I'm reassured of it all. I see you there, and I feel like no matter what I'm gonna do, it won't matter, I can't do it wrong. That's all I need," he said looking into the ocean. "It must be something you do to me in your sleep."

"I don't do things in my sleep," she said in her little voice.

"Hmmm, I don't know, that just might not be true."

Addie wrapped an arm around Page's back as they sat quietly. She rested her head on his bony bicep. "I'm tie-ohd," she said.

"I know," he said putting his cheek on her head. "It's cold here babe, let's go back."

"What do you think is the cure for world hunger? Sharing? Do you think sharing will do it?" Page asked raising an eyebrow.

"Yeah, I think sharing would go a long way," Longwell replied plainly. "Sharing, and cutting the throats of a few billionaires, distributing their money out to poor people."

Page ignored the latter comment and lit a cigarette. "No, sharing isn't gonna do shit. It's not even gonna ever happen, so those stupid people waiting might as well go ahead and quit holding their breath. You'll turn blue in the face waiting for that shit." Page flicked his nose. "As long as people have been alive, there's been some poor motherfucker dying 'cus he's got nothing to eat. To think, all of a sudden, humans are going to start sharing at a level significant enough to end world hunger is just plain ignoring the facts of history, facts of humans too. It's unprecedented shit. Now I agree that if people were to miraculously start sharing more, giving more, un-Scroogeing, then, yeah, maybe we could save a couple lives here and there, but even so, that's not gonna completely stop people from starving. Nobody starving? Shit, you know how many people there are?

Longwell blew his breath out after a hiccup.

"There's always gonna be some douche in East Africa living on top of a fucking rock, sitting there dying by himself. Just earlier today, Discovery Channel showed something where this African guy had to walk three miles just to go get a bucket full of water. And he had to carry back this filled bucket, no lid or nothing, carrying it on top of his head, you know? And he's trying his best to make sure he doesn't spill any. Hoping that way there'll be enough leftover, after his family drinks enough to not fucking die of dehydration – so they can wash his baby sister," Page sniffed, "'Cus she smells like shit. They share a bed, and he can't sleep 'cus she's so fucking gross smelling curled up next to him. Why's she smell like shit? 'Cus she's been sittin' in shit – all day. You gonna tell me there's not enough money going around to at least buy this kid a piece of Tupperware? Like 99 cents. Put the lid on it, keep the water in no problem. Clean the shit off his sister, get a good night's sleep. Is that too much to ask? No. Nobody gives a fuck."

"Alright, why don't you take a couple more puffs of that cigarette," Longwell said holding up his hand. "Christ, calm down."

"I'm fine."

Addie smoked her cigarette too. She remained quiet. Straight from the beach, they'd come to the Fish Kettle for a drink and had run into Colander, Longwell, McGee, and a few other friends. As she tapped the cigarette end to release some ash, an older gentleman she knew well walked through the doors.

"Dante the Greek, what are you doing here? How are you? How are you?" she repeated standing up and giving him a hug. "Hmmm, it's so good to see you."

"Oh, my dear Addie. You sweet girl," he said hugging her back.

Dante wasn't Greek, but had spent the better part of one of his decades in its heat and whenever he went out he wore the hat of the country's fishermen. Addie added "the Greek" to his name whenever she saw him. His old grey hair and weathered skin had taken the brunt of his age and wrinkles cut his face.

"What have you been doing?" she asked.

"Who, me? Oh, nothing. I'm just trying to figure out if it's going to be – heaven or hell," he joked.

"You're the sweetest man alive. How could you have any question about it?"

"Oh – oh, you. Come here," he wrapped his arms around her neck and gave the girl a kiss on the forehead. "You know you're a good kid." He greeted the others at the table as he sat down with them. It didn't take long into a drink before he began to tell one of his stories. The table quieted.

"So I needed a date for this show my buddies and I wanted to go to. Now back then in Greece, they had the best damn performers of the time playing in these theatres. Which by the way, the theatres, they were built back in the ancient times. Some great looking shit. The whole thing made out of beautifully carved rock. Granite? I don't know, probably not. The place was still comfortable, still current technologically. But they never charged much to go see the best. It had nothing to do with the money. If the performer was one of the best of the time, they wanted to make sure everybody could see them. Poor, rich, whatever. You needed to be able to see this person, and they let you. This was your entertainer!" Dante said raising his hands. "Not like today."

Colander reached to the table for his drink, and everyone else waited motionless for the man to continue.

"So I needed a date. Not gonna show up without one," he took a sip to re-wet his lips. "All my friends already had their girls so I had to go looking for mine. Luckily, right down the street from where we were living was the best whorehouse you'll ever see. I mean the best. Even this guy," Dante pointed at Colander. "Even he'd be doing a beauty. Top notch girls."

The table laughed.

"So I go in there and find me the prettiest looking one I can. A real knockout. I'm telling you, she was in bloom. The ripest. Anyways, I go and meet my friends at the theatre – in our seats. I told them before that I'd just meet them there. So I'm walking down the aisle, and I got this beauty on my arm. Now every man's head we pass is turning to keep their stare of her. You know, their necks twisting and chins slumping," he twisted and slumped. "I had the best looking girl in the whole damn place!" the Greek paused to smile. He clapped his hands together and pushed his glasses back up his nose – very happy with himself. "I sit down with my friends, introduce them all to her, and they're all bug-eyed looking at me, mouths wide open. And I say, 'Hey! You let those drooling tongues drop one bit on her, and you best bet you're paying for that. She's costing me a goddamn fortune as is!'"

The entire table laughed.

"That's some funny stuff," Longwell said a little too quickly. He motioned to the waitress and called for a refill. "I wish we had a good whorehouse."

"Eww. That is disgusting," Addie said. "Those girls are a walking infestation. Probably so loose it's just falling out."

"You could use a little loosening yourself there, lady," Longwell came back.

She gave him the finger.

"Alright you two," Page intervened. "Need a bullet-proof wall between them."

"I wouldn't leave those two alone with a gun in the room," Colander said bringing his glass to his mouth.

Neither said anything more to each other, and a few hours passed. Dante sat up in his chair, itched above his lip, and then emptied the cup down his throat. "Well, I'm afraid that's it for me kids. Time to go on home. I just don't have the same energy I used to – that you strapping youths are filled with – taking it so for granted, you guys," he put his hand on Page's shoulder and gave a squeeze. He threw a couple dollars down onto the table and stood up. "You go ask the beauty I had that night though – the gorgeous whore – she'll tell you all about how late I could go. Twice in the morning too. Hey!" He pumped his fist.

"Dante!" Addie shouted.

"Sorry, sorry. I know you didn't need to hear that, dear," he said shuffling over to her. He kissed the top of her head.

"God, I hope you brushed your teeth since then," Addie said giving him a grossed-out face.

"Always a smartass. That's why I like you," he grabbed a hold of her cheek for a second. "Now you all take care of yourselves and remember – there's plenty to go around for everyone, but nobody's there handing it to you."

They all said their goodbyes and Dante left, tipping his hat to the maitre d' at the door. There was a noticeable quiet around the table. Everyone stared off and waited.

"So I finally got a toothbrush with a big head again," Page said leaning over to Colander. "That small one was killing me."

"Oh, yeah. You gotta get the big head," Colander replied.

"Yeah, I just can't get around to everything as well with the small one. You know? You can feel it getting only half your tooth, but then the big one covers everything. The whole thing."

"Yep, exactly."

Page stared at his glass. "It's got the massaging of the gums thing too," he said, circling his finger around his mouth. "Feels great."

Colander laughed. "Yeah, I've seen the commercial for those I think."

"Oral-B," Page said taking a puff of his cigarette.

"Oh, I'm a Crest man."

"Crest? Nice."

Everyone from the table had left but Longwell. The night had grown, and when six o'clock in the same place every night becomes midnight, only a select few can overcome the sluggishness. Longwell was sitting now in a booth. Across from him was a friend, Steph. The two had been involved so far in nothing more than conversation. It was a simple relationship based solely on one another's mutual respect for the other's youthful attitude. Youthful, carefree, reckless – whatever. She was a lesbian, and he thought that was cool too.

Steph had slim muscle in all sorts of places, and there was just enough of her to grab onto in her head or wherever else you like. Her hair fell on her back in light brown curls, and her cheeks plumped up to make her nose look a little smaller than it really was.

"It's late. You're just now getting here?" Longwell asked well-in, but still up.

"Long day at work," she said. She wore shorts, and underneath her bare legs, she inserted her hands. "The old man I work for, Mr. Figgleman, his house is huge so it takes awhile to clean everything," she explained.

"I see."

"Guy's filthy rich. His father made a fortune from Standard Oil. Apparently one of their bigwigs. He died soon after, left all the money to his son – this Figgleman. Guy's a cheap bastard, he just sits on his money. Hardly spends anything on anybody. Anyways, he's a senile fuck. He's the only one who lives there, and every week I come in and his house is a complete mess. Newspapers thrown all around his study, food he's dropped onto the floor and left all week, tea kettles sitting out on tables, and every time a huge stack of plates, silverware, and glasses sitting in the sink. Then he makes me hand-wash them! He has a dishwasher."

Longwell snickered.

"So today I said,"

"Mr. Figgleman, you have a dishwasher!" she said patronizing him and presenting the dishwasher with a gesture of her hands. "Don't you see it here? Why do I have to wash these by hand?"

"You keep those lips rested for your butch-haired girlfriend." Figgleman did not beat around the bush.

"What?" Her hands were still gesturing the dishwasher.

"Muff-muncher," he mumbled under his breath, and then left the room under the aid of his walker.

"What did you just call me?" She asked with her voice raised loudly, her hands on the back of her hips now, and her neck shooting forward. But he didn't hear it.

"He's one crazy old man," she said to Longwell while bringing a hand up to flick something out of her eyelash. She kept the hand out and gripped her beer bottle.

"Why would you even work for this prick?"

"Because he's rich! I figured the old fuck would at least pay well. Cheap bastard."

Longwell nodded without a word, spitting the ice back into his glass.

"But here's the thing. After he left the kitchen, I went and checked out the dishwasher. Opened the thing up, and out falls piles of cash. Right out onto the kitchen floor. The whole thing's filled with money! No lock on the door or anything."

"Are you serious?"

"He's keeping a huge stash of his millions in his goddamn dishwasher, right there in the middle of his kitchen."

"What a crazy old man."

"Like I said, a senile fuck."

Longwell began aggressively poking-out the late-night dinner he'd had from in-between his teeth. Lettuce bits and bacon-bites, using nothing but his tongue to get them out. "I take it – it wouldn't be too tough to get in," he suggested.

Steph reached into her pocket, pulled out a set of keys, and dangled them above the table. "I *am* the loyal maid," she said smiling.

The Portuguese waiter came over to the table, "Last call," he said.

One of the bus boys was out on the sidewalk breaking down the tables. He folded each leg in quickly so as to not be in the cold air for long. He stacked the chairs up on one another, and then carried the outside dining area into a winter storage room, piece by piece.

"25 percent," she demanded, sticking her neck out like before.

"15," Longwell countered, nearly caught off guard.

She slowly began to bring the key back to her pocket.

"Bitch. Alright, 25."

"Ha-ha. Here," she threw him the key. "Now buy me another beer before this place closes."

"What?"

She tilted her head, made a big smile and batted her eyelashes. Longwell caved and clumsily slid out of the booth.

"I suppose I could use one too – get me whiskey or something." He pulled money from his pocket and started counting it. "You know, I don't know why I'm so nice to some girl that's never gonna sleep with me."

"In the back of your mind, you think one day I'll let you watch," she said and took one of her bottle's last swigs.

Longwell hiccupped, shook his finger in the air, and without a word headed to the bar for the drinks.

Midway through the next day's afternoon, Colander took one step out of his building, turned around, and went back inside. Hassled, he walked up the staircase to the second floor, went into his room, grabbed his jacket, and then came back outside again. He stood right by the door, putting together the buttons and looking up and down the street for anything suspicious. He walked to the sidewalk. Satisfied though still on guard, he checked down the alleyway, extending by just the neck to curl his head around the corner.

After the brief walk, Colander joined his two friends at the Fish Kettle. Back there again, for Longwell it was as if he never left. The afternoon's conversation was interrupted by a cell phone ring coming from the table next to them. Its servant came to its call, and after ripping through his bag's contents, he surfaced with the phone in hand. The phone had a strange bulk to it, was obtrusively large, and not in accordance with the time's mini-fad.

"Hey, it's Zack Morris calling, says he wants his phone back," Longwell joked.

"Yeah? How'd he call then?" Colander challenged.

Longwell shook his head and let out a loud

breath.

Colander continued, "Did Kelly and the gang band together, scheme some adorable plan to raise money and buy Zack a new phone? A mini-phone now. All this, of course, coming with a couple laughs at the expense of Screech."

"Kelly's fucking hot," Longwell noted.

"I'm more a Jessie guy myself. I dig the brains," Colander decided and said so leaning out of his seat.

Page stared at the ice in his cup. The cubes melted in their own puddle.

"Saved – by – the bell," Longwell slowly let out.

"Long legs," Colander continued.

A dark haired girl sat in a booth with the backend of a spoon against her tooth. She flicked her fingers into the hair strands that fell down on her face. Her seat put her directly in Page's view. The soup she ate was chicken pea, and the spoon left her mouth clean each time. A pear sat up on its bottom to the right of the bowl, and out its top grew a stout brown stem, its insides plumped the center. Page abruptly pushed out of his chair and headed over to her.

"I don't mean to interrupt you, but I can't help to notice you're eating soup with a pear and, well, that's the strangest combinations I think I've ever seen."

She pulled the spoon out of her mouth clean. Puckered her lips tight as if pecking, and gave the stranger a look up and down. "The coolness of the pear puts the soup's heat out. It's a good mix," she hung on the word *mix*, not on purpose, but as if her mouth tripped – a lisp really. She caught it instantly, and her eyes darted to the table. "I have lazy lips – I mean tongue," she said and laughed nervously. "Only sometimes though".

"Oh, I do nearly everything sometimes."

"Is that right?" she asked taking another spoonful.

"Yeah," Page came back assuredly. "But I don't really have that much to do anyways."

"Well here, take a bite of this pear," she said offering it up with her hand. It was full but a bite. "There's something to do."

Page took a bite and then the seat across from her, the pear still in his hand, his bite edging next to hers.

"What is your name?"

"Sara."

"Hi Sara,"

"Sara Marie Lynn."

"Aww." Page nodded. "I'm Page."

"Hello Page," she said spooning up some soup, and offering him the utensil.

"Oh, no thank you. I'll stick to the pear."

"Alright, suit yourself. You're missing the combination," she said, and brought the spoon into her mouth. "I have a question to ask you, Page."

"Already?" he said mocking misery.

"Yes, Mr. Page. You cannot come sit down here, take bites into my pear, bat those eyes at me, all without being questioned – no way, no how,"

"Ok, fair enough." He took another bite of the pear, swallowed, and waited, intrigued.

"Are you angry about something? You seem angry."

"What?"

"I saw how you were looking over there," she pointed towards his table of friends, wiggling her spoon. "All gruff."

"Gruff? I'm not angry," Page crumpled his lips with his fingers, and then said, "I'm delightful."

She stole the fruit back from his hand.

"Ha-ha. De-light-ful," she sounded out the word while smiling at her pear, stumbling on the 'ful'. She stared deeply at him for a moment. "I'll believe you. You know, pears are my favorite fruit," she added.

"How come?"

"When I take a bite," and she did, "the taste, it dances down my tongue." Half-chewed chunks spit out as she began to laugh. Her palm cupped her mouth. She was not embarrassed, and Page began to laugh as well.

"I like pears too." Page stole the fruit back from her. She made a sad face. "But I've never seen one dance before."

"They don't dance – dummy. The flavor, it just moves," she said while making waves with her voice to synch with the up and down gestures of her hand.

"I don't know what you're talking about," Page kidded her.

"Dude. Forget it," she tried to sound mad, but laughed at herself with elbows on the table.

"Do you like drugs?" Page asked excitedly.

"No, I eat chocolate."

"Huh? What do you mean?"

"My friends and I, yesterday, spent a day eating chocolate."

"Just chocolate? Why'd you do that?"

"Because it's good, man. Don't you like chocolate?" she asked wiping her eyes.

Page laughed. "Well, yeah. Chocolate, I like, but-"

"Well, chocolate does me good. If you like drugs and that does you good, well then that's fine. Enjoy. Bon appetit."

Page scratched the back of his head and moved his eyes around the Fish Kettle's walls, all quite blankly. She took a strand of hair by its end and kept it in her puckered lips.

Page tried to think of something else to say. "So what were you doing before you came in here?"

"Can't say. It ain't right," she answered quickly and without looking up.

"What?"

She laughed softly, and then came with the truth. "No I was just in my apartment, right up on the west side. I got hungry so I came here. I like the soup – and the pears."

"I didn't even know they served soup here. This place, huh? How come I've never seen you here before?"

"How should I know?" she asked raising her shoulders. "I come here," she said and took a bite out of the pear, "just not when you do," her mouth was open wide and she said her words pear-filled.

"You know, you're full of funny faces."

"Funny faces?"

"Yeah. Your face talks for you the best. It's clear you don't properly know how to use your mouth."

She said nothing and instead arched her eyebrows, stared her eyes, and made the unconscious look of considering.

"There, see," Page said smiling. "You just said something."

"Yeah? What I say?" she asked without breaking the look.

"I don't know," Page calmly admitted. "I don't understand the face. I speak in tongue."

She said nothing and her look cracked into a bit of a smile. "My tongue doesn't work. I told you." She took a spoonful of soup, and then said, "I once saw a person, he had so many piercings in his tongue, he'd take out the studs and pull his tongue up like this," she took hold of her tongue, and with her fingers brought it up to just below her nose.

Page began to laugh.

"Den he coul' play id jus' like a flutttte." She dropped her tongue. "He did the National Anthem when I saw him."

"No shit. The whole National Anthem?"

"It didn't sound that great," she admitted, stumbling on the word *great.* She began to laugh, and then buried her nose in her shoulder.

"Yeah, well what about you? What is it you're doing with yourself? How do you play a flute?"

"No flute," she paused. "I'm studying to be a meteor-ologis-is."

"Weather, huh?"

"Weather."

"That's interesting. A nice investment too, it'll always be there."

"Investment? What you talking about?" She didn't wait for him to answer. "No, I'll be a very good mete-orol-o-giss. What about you? What are you doing here?"

Page held back a response. He looked down at the table and scratched behind his ear. "I'm here – uh – talking to you, I guess. I was talking to them," he said pointing to his friends.

Sara gave an unsatisfied look.

"Well, I used to flirt in the business of consolidating temporary, uh, equilaterally drawn and imported – I told you, I don't do that much anymore, but I used to."

"Ahhh, a bum who does nothing? And a very informative, thorough, and clear one at that. Straight forward and outright."

Page laughed behind his hand. "I'm not a bum. I live comfortably. My ends meet," he said with his face buried in his palm, one eye scrunched closed, and the other on Sara. His elbow on the table propped his head up, and she could see only half his smile behind his cloaking hand.

"Well maybe you should start doing things again," she offered and took the last bite of the pear. "My food's gone," she said and dropped the spoon into her empty bowl.

"Oh," he said trying to figure what to make of that. He came out from behind his hand.

Back at the other table, Longwell asked, "Where'd Page go?"

"He's over there talking to that chick," Colander answered.

"What chick?" he asked turning to see. "Oh, she's getting up," a silent hiccup made Longwell pause. "Musta blown it," he said letting out his breath.

"So when am I going to ever see you again?" Page asked.

"You may not. Truth is, I'm leaving town in a couple days, moving away."

"What? Stay, stick around."

"No, I'm past this."

"Where you moving to?"

"Down south."

"Well what's going on in those couple days you're still here?"

"End of school. Me-tea-orol-ogy. I have two finals in two days. I can't have you around. I got the studying to do. I can tell already you like to suck up time," she said and tapped him on the end of his nose.

"So this is it? I'm never going to see you again?"

"'Dats all, maybe"

Page nodded. "Then that's how it is, huh?"

Sara's mouth clicked. "Yep, I know," she said raising her shoulders and letting out a deep breath. She struggled to reach her hand into the pocket of her tight jeans. As she brought her hand out, it pushed up the bottom of her shirt, and Page caught a glimpse of her hip and its pale skin. She dropped a couple singles and wadded the rest back into her pocket. "Well you know my name, look me up whenever you want to. Come find me."

"My only hint is that you're south of here?"

"Phonebook, silly. Sara Marie Lynn. You can find that, I promise. I wouldn't think there's an insurmountable number of us south of you. I do hope to see you again, Mr. Page. You know how to see a lady through her pear and soup." She brushed her hand atop his shoulder and walked away. Page stayed in the booth until she had gone out the door.

"Well boys, out of the tree of life, I just picked me a plum," Page said sitting back in his chair at the table.

"What are you talking about?" Colander asked. "I thought she was eating a pear."

"It's Sinatra, man."

Colander's face tightened, and he thought for a second.

"That girl I was sitting with over there – she likes those pears 'cus the flavors dance down her tongue."

"What the fuck does that mean?" Longwell asked.

Page raised his shoulders, and made a face as if he didn't know either.

Longwell leaned to the side of his chair to try and get a better look of Sara. She was still on the sidewalk outside the Fish Kettle's window.

"She is eating her hair right now," Longwell remarked.

"She's not eating it. She just puts it in her mouth."

"Oh, she has oral fixations?" Longwell asked with a smirk.

"Shut up," Page replied smiling.

Longwell turned back to face the table. "Well

I'd put it in her," he said as he picked a sunflower shell off his tongue with a finger.

"That's nice to know," Page replied.

"Too bad about Addie though, huh?" Longwell added. He threw some more seeds in.

"No," Page said simply. "Not too bad."

Addie sat with her legs crossed tightly, and her fingertips being nibbled in her mouth. Her black hoody was zipped, and hair pulled back save the strands hanging aside her cheek. A skinny white slice was all that was not covered by her pupil, her skin yellowed and she giggled.

"I can't feel my face."

Her friend laughed. "It'll come back," her friend, Sue-Ellen, said that without a look up.

Addie laughed again. The waitress set down two tea cups, and put the kettle in the middle of the table. The girls sat with a tiny table in-between them. The coffeehouse was on the east side, nearly across from Page's apartment. Most everyone in there was scholarly, glasses wearing, and typing on their laptops.

"Can I smoke in here?" Addie asked.

"Sure," the waitress answered. Sue-Ellen poured both of them the tea she'd delivered. The steam jumped out of the cup, hit the otherwise immeasurable passing breeze, and took off in it. Addie watched it go.

"So what did you want to talk about?" Sue-Ellen asked.

Addie's head jerked up from the cup, and her

eyes came upon her friend. Sue-Ellen was knitting herself a hat. The yarn's end weaved up between two wooden sticks, and its ball unraveled in her lap. She held the half-knit hat up to judge it for size and show. The girl had friendly round eyes that stood at the tips of her smile.

"Oh. Well. The thing is – what it boils down to – is that," she stopped and sighed. "I don't know what to ever take seriously anymore." She became immediately quiet.

"What do you mean? What did you take seriously before?" Sue-Ellen replied without looking up – her eyes, she kept on the yarn.

Addie's fingers stayed still on her lips. She tried to remember what she used to think about before, and what she before considered to be a serious matter. She couldn't help but start to laugh. "That's just it. I couldn't tell you one thing I used to think before! I don't have a clue," she said as if surrendering with her hands up. She sat back in the chair and uncrossed her legs. "There came a day where I felt no relation to my past self. No connection with that person at all. I could tell you nothing about her. There's nothing to me that came before this present moment, there is, I know, but nothing that I can grab on to. That person from before stopped existing to me. If I try to think back even five minutes ago, and define the person who just right then was in front of you, sipping tea, I become terrified. Extremely uncomfortable in feeling any tie with me and the person before me. Me."

Sue-Ellen glanced up and sympathetically smiled, her attention then returned to the yarn.

"And the fact that I wouldn't even know where to start something as simple as coming up with traits to define myself, I just – how is that? It's so exhausting," Addie stopped and began to scratch her cheek. "Maybe it was a gradual process. I can't remember. The day it happened must have blurred into the others."

"There's no reason you should feel you have to connect with that person," Sue-Ellen said looking up at Addie and weaving a stitch blind. "How could that person still exist? Our brain is constantly taking things in, and at a rate that changes us too quickly for any hope of catching up to it. The past Addie is some fragment in a couple people's memories, and as you said," she stuck her tongue out to guide the needle through. "Not yours," she looked back down to check her hat. "She's not a real person, Addie. She was. Once you are beyond the present mind, there is no defining."

"She is real to some people," Addie said looking straight at her friend. Sue-Ellen's long fingers moved gracefully, and the control in which she displayed while weaving her yarn impressed Addie. "I suppose you're right though," she continued. "I don't know where I see my past-self. It's not in my eyes. I feel forced to try and find her." Addie started nibbling again.

"Family, old friends, sometimes. They cling to whichever vision of you that'll make them the happiest.

They liked you how you were. They see the new you and don't know how to take it, their minds then bring up your old profile."

Addie foraged through her bag for a cigarette.

"How does this look?" Sue-Ellen held up her hat, the sewing needles still hanging.

"I like it."

Sue-Ellen smiled at the hat, and then put it back down on her lap. "Anyways, as I was saying, the feeling is all too human. But there are certain thoughts that you shouldn't think about. Certain realities that you never want to not blindly accept. Trying to disbelieve them or challenge them leads you nowhere but swirling down. That bus is there, this hat is here. There are challenges you can raise to that, but why would you want to? It leads to more questions than answers. I know that's cowardly, but we've been given too much pasture in which to roam. Some things just aren't worth confronting daily. Not worth worrying about. They'll bury you."

Addie had her right hand gripping the top of her skull, the left wrapped around the back of her neck. The cigarette was unlit in her lips. She pulled her arms in opposite directions, gently, so she could feel the tension in her neck, and her eyes widened. She made a quiet grunting sound. Sue-Ellen turned her hat inside out, plopped it down loosely onto her head, puffed it up and smiled.

Old man Figgleman's house was a couple streets down from Huntington. This pleased Longwell, as he did not want to commit any criminal action so close to where he cavorted. You do not shit where you eat, but at the same time there isn't anyone you wouldn't shit on. To a man like Longwell, there is nobody below the line and nobody above, all people are right next to each other. Everyone's a degenerate. And if there is some fool's head to be stepped on and the price is right, Longwell's already worked out his boost. Surely, he is not alone in this world of head crunching, groin shot, eye poking. But was he alone? Yes, he was alone.

The night wasn't quite cold, but Longwell wore an overcoat. The coat served more to the purpose of concealing the bulging trash bag, full of the money he anticipated, than it did to keep him from a chill. The empty bag, he had stuffed in one of the coat pockets, along with a black wooly mask and a knife with a half foot long blade, just in case. He walked quickly though not straight. It was nearly midnight, and there was not a nearly midnight that he'd been sober since he could remember.

He took the scrap of paper out that he had

written Figgleman's address on, and checked it to the number on the face of the building. He put it back in his pant-pocket and came out with the key.

The townhouse Figgleman lived in was quaint, and its bottom floor consisted of multiple, small, sitting rooms. Each room was heavily decorated for such a bachelor, though perhaps it should be chalked up to the old man in Figgleman for being such a crap collector. Every room's décor could be likened to a waiting room's. There were small, nearly uncomfortable, couches with coffee tables in front of them, and along the walls were standing chests, desks, and armoires. In the chests and on the desks were Figgleman's collections of crap. Insignificant awards that took shape in statues, plaques, engraved glasses, and plates, they donned the desktops and were somewhere to keep the dust. Antique vases and goblets, even a chunky suit of armor or two, all this made up old man Figgleman's downstairs decorations. And all these things he was quite proud of. It was in these rooms that he entertained his few afternoon guests, and would at his leisure point the conversation towards his such and such award, given for excellence, brilliancy, or exemplary performance in a long ago such and such.

Longwell could see nearly none of this in the night's darkness. He crouched low and started waddling toward the gut of the house in search of its kitchen. His hand gripped table-top to table-top. He crossed a threshold into another room. No kitchen, another room's entrance in front of him. Longwell let out an annoyed groan. He rose slightly out of his squat to see beyond a couch and into the next room. A light flicked on in the room he scouted, illuminating a counter, a stove-top, and a faucet curved into the sink.

In the kitchen, Figgleman moved gingerly on his walker from the cupboard to the fridge. He had set a glass down on the counter, and now shut the fridge's door with a container of prune juice taken from it. He reached around and set the juice on the counter behind him, took hold of the walker, and pivoted back around to the empty glass. Longwell sat quietly, patiently waiting for the man to wet his old encrusted mouth, relieve himself in the bathroom probably, and then get on back to bed.

Figgleman leaned with one hand on the walker and one on the counter. His glass was a quarter gone when he began to hear the unusual sound of human hiccups. Knowing them not to be coming from him, he turned to the offensive, set his juice down, and took-on his walker, completely unafraid.

Longwell hiccupped again, his hand covering his mouth. Another one came, and launched his shoulders up uncontrollably. He shook his head in disbelief at such timing and became nervous of being found out, though against such a debilitated foe, he felt himself to be well prepared. He waited for what may come with his hand around the knife's handle.

Figgleman moved in small chunks towards

the living room adjacent to his kitchen. Longwell had maneuvered to the couch's front, its back to the kitchen. He was bent between the sofa and the coffee table, and was in a position that afforded him a view of the oncoming old man, though there was no way, especially with the elder's lagging eyesight, that Figgleman could see him. Longwell hiccupped again, and Figgleman heard it.

The creak of the old man leaning on his walker became louder as he neared the backside of the couch. There was light coming in from the kitchen, but unwilling to compromise his illusions on the element of surprise, Figgleman did not turn any light on in the living room. He preferred stalking in the dark.

Now right up against the back of the couch, Figgleman honed in on his target, a body he perceived. He lifted the walker above his head. "Mongrel!" He shouted, and swung the thing down as hard as he could. The walker struck only against the coffee table, and Figgleman flipped over the back of the couch, first landing on the cushions, and then tumbling down to the same space in-between the couch and coffee table that Longwell had just scrambled from. Lying stuck on his back, the old man let out a painful moan.

Now up at the couch's side, Longwell took frantic breaths, trying to catch his cool. He hiccupped again.

"Ahhhh, my back," Figgleman shrieked. The old man was stuck there on the floor, had no chance of moving. His stiff body was no longer responding, and Longwell was quick to notice this, and even quicker to make a break for the dishwasher.

"You chicken shit! Stealing from a poor old man!"

"Fuck you."

Figgleman began to work himself up into a frenzy, as the crash of the dishwasher-door being flung open and the snap of a trash bag being pumped in the air came from his kitchen. Longwell peeked inside and saw the stacks of green reaching from the bottom of the dishwasher to its top. The towers of money continuing all the way from the washer's front to its back.

"Oh shit - look at all that money," Longwell said laughing to himself.

"What's your name thief? I demand you tell me your name!"

"Andrew Horgan," Longwell called back with a wide grin. He began shoveling money into his trash bag.

"Fool! I have you now! Do you know what I can do with just a name? I'm unsure that you are even worthy of matching-up against my wits, now! I will pity you, Andrew Horgan. Once you are caught in my clutches, it'll be an entire hell, good sir, of which you've brought upon yourself! It'll have no end, no limit, no pause, no play, no rewind, no fast forward button, no, ahhhh," Figgleman had lost his train of thought.

"You senile fuck."

"Base insult, crazy is neither here nor there. You have made a powerful enemy tonight! Are you aware of the actions I'm capable of?" he asked from his backside.

"Yeah let's hear it, guy. I could use a couple laughs while stealing your shit."

There was a moment before his response. "Money is shit," he finally said. Then another silent pause. "But the money is *mine*," he stated emphatically and with a striking finger pointed at the ceiling. "I happen to be a close acquaintance of a one Mr. J. Edgar Hoover. Ah-ha! Does that name strike fear in you, son?"

"J. Edgar Hoover? That strikes in me vacuuming."

"J. Edgar is more of a *man* than you will ever be!" He yelled wiggling his pointed finger some more. "And if he's even half as tenacious a *man*-hunter as I hear him to be, well then Mr. Horgan, he will be in your underpants faster than you can say, 'Turn on, tune in, drop out.' you cockgobblin' hippie."

Longwell was belly deep in the dishwasher, and his laughter echoed within the metal confines. With the money in there too, there was hardly any other room. His laughter slowed the robbery, but he was already down to the last stack. Longwell moved fast. "Oh man, you are something else," he said shaking his head, grabbing the last bills. "What does some old fuck like you need this money for anyways? You aren't doing anything to deserve it. Your ass and mouth clearly shit just the same," Longwell said and then stood up. He hoisted the trash bag over his shoulder and swung the door of the empty dishwasher up with his foot. "So, you know what? Fuck you – the money is *mine* actually,"

"You will pay for this." Figgleman's voice was beginning to wobble. He had still not gotten a good look of the thief's face. The living room was far too dark, and he didn't once see Longwell while he was in the kitchen's light, as the couch blocked his view, but still Figgleman's stubbornness convinced him he would recognize any man who'd robbed him. "I will find you," he vowed.

"No, probably not," Longwell said stepping by Figgleman and making his way for the door. "Oh, don't get up, I'll show myself out," he said turning back to Figggleman. He looked forward again and came another grin. Longwell opened the front door, and walked right out.

Figglemen made a muttering sound to himself, and had the foresight to cozy-in to his paralyzed position on the hard wood floor.

"You dress too nice," Addie said to Page.

"Too nice? I thought I was a ragamuffin?"

The two walked through the brisk morning air and approached Huntington Street's corner bends from the east.

"Yeah, well. You're a confused little boy."

The south bend was just ahead of them when, around its corner, turned a triumphant young Chocolate Lab puppy. Tail wagging, and its extended leash pulling behind him, his owner still remained unseen, blocked from the couple's view by the Rickety Shell, a seafood place. The dog sat on the bend's corner, staring across the street, impatiently in wait of its owner. Right as Addie saw the dog, she smiled and rushed towards him.

"Oh I just wanna kiss you all over. Yes, come here and I will kiss you," Addie spoke in her little voice and wiggled her fingers in the air as if to tickle. The dog turned, stamped his feet on the ground, looked with his ears up, and seemed to smile in his pant. He waddled the two more feet towards Addie that his leash would allow.

"I want to love you," she said hugging him. Her

shoulder pushed the dog's snout up, and he licked her cheek and the inside of her ear. "Oh yes, look at you," she oozed, petting him all over. "I would eat you. Yes, I would."

Page stood waiting over them. After a slight smile at the two, he ran his hand along the dog's back once, and then looked on down the street. On the other side of the bend, the dog's owner was mid-conversation, seeming to be oblivious to her arm being pulled by the leash.

"Look at that stupid bitch," Addie said standing up. "She doesn't give a shit about her dog."

"Ok, let's go," Page said prodding her along.

"Take care of your dog, lady!" she yelled, and then bent down to pet him goodbye. She began to ooze again. "Alright, yes, we have to go, little buddy. You bite that bitch whenever you want. Ok? Bye-bye."

They began walking again, and as they passed the dog's owner they overheard the woman informing an acquaintance, "oh, yes well my psychiatrist says that I should get out more often, walk the dog, you know, mingle with the people. She said dogs make you happy. It is supposed to help the quivering," she explained, shook a little bit then brought her fingers to her mouth. She looked up and down the street. "I've never seen this place before, though it seems just downright marvelous."

Addie turned around and spit at the woman's feet.

Page grabbed her by the elbow and pulled her to make sure that was the end of it. "Come on, you," he said. "Let's go get some breakfast. I'm hungry."

Colander was hungry too. He had already flipped his pancake, and its second side would soon be cooked. He transferred it onto a plate, and set his breakfast down on the table. The noontime sun was coming through his kitchen window, and the breakfast smells were turning his empty stomach over. He sat down, and his fork he picked up, when he heard a commotion going on outside his door.

"Hey, what are you doing? Get back here!" a woman screamed.

Colander looked up from his plate and listened from his chair.

From the hallway, the woman began shouting, "Call the police!"

Colander's face hardened and he took the napkin out of his lap, dropped the fork, and headed for his door. He looked through the peephole but could see nothing, so he swung the door open to stick his head out.

Other tenants had come out of their apartments, and gathered to see what the woman was screaming about. Colander, in his pajama pants and bed riddled hair, walked barefoot over to the huddle of people just a bit further down the hall from his apartment. He saw that the woman who had screamed was the building's superintendent, and he came upon the other tenants standing around her and a ladder just as she began to tell what had happened.

"There was a man!" she explained with her hands raised. "He was right here using this ladder. He must have broken into the closet. I know it was locked. I always lock it," she explained and pushed her way through somebody to get to the closet door. "See, look at the door!"

Next to the door knob, the wood had clearly been damaged by a crowbar or the like.

"When I came down the hall, he was up on the ladder, messing around with the smoke alarm," she said walking back into the middle of the group and pointing up to the ceiling. "Did anybody call the cops? I don't know where he went. He saw me, and ran off that way down the hall," she pointed in the direction of Colander's apartment, and inadvertently directly at him. The entire group turned to see him standing there with the sleep still in his eyes. He sniffed once, and stared back at them.

"I didn't see anybody," he said. Behind him, his door stood wide-open.

From the opposite side of the hall, a gentleman came rushing back to the group. "I've called the police," he announced nearly out of breath. "They're sending someone over soon."

The group began mumbling amongst themselves.

"Why the smoke alarm?" one person asked another.

"What if they've planted a bomb?"

"It's all these youngsters come into the neighborhood. What they bring with them is no good," an old-timer said.

"That's a sweeping generalization," a young woman answered her.

"Hmmph," the old lady said back.

One of the young male tenants turned to his buddy, "Osama-fuckin' Bin-laden, man," he said slapping his hand into the other palm.

"Dude, you don't know what you are talking about. He's got – a major beard, a big fluffy hat, and the lanky fucker's like six foot four – he probably wouldn't even need the ladder," the buddy speculated.

Colander turned around and headed back for his pancakes. He shuffled around his open door, walked in, and closed it behind him. The smell of his pancakes reached and enticed him. But upon sitting at the kitchen table, he noticed his fork had gone missing. It no longer was beside his plate. He got up and saw it wasn't in the sink either. Colander turned around and pondered over his pancake. He was surprised to see his kitchen window open, and he didn't think it to be him who had spilled the syrup that now streamed down the side of his counter and ran onto his floor.

About ten minutes later, he came out of his apartment fully dressed. A police officer was up on the very same ladder the assailant had used, checking over the smoke alarm. The superintendent was standing below at the ladder's foot, nervously watching the policeman. Colander approached.

"Well, looks like we're all set here," the officer told her.

"You found nothing? No signs of tampering?"

"Nope. Looks like he just stole the batteries. Going to have to put in new ones to meet city code," he said coming down the ladder.

"Shouldn't the fire department be the ones handling something like this?" Colander asked.

The superintendent jumped back, startled by Colander's presence, but then she looked back to the police officer.

"No," he said.

Inside the smoke alarm, a foreign red light clicked on, and a robotic noise hummed with the movement of a tiny camera.

Over the officer's radio came, "10-95, we need you. We got a 507 in progress."

"10-4," he said back. "I'm sorry, ma'am but I have to go," he excused himself and picked his tools up.

"Can I assume my insurance will cover the batteries?" the woman asked.

"Probably not. Small price for batteries, not

exactly worth the paperwork," the officer answered, pushing by them.

"What if we added a fork?" Colander asked.

"Hey, Longwell," the Fish Kettle waitress called while walking towards him. "There's a message here for you."

"For me?"

"Yeah, you want another drink?"

"Yeah," he nodded. She dropped the message onto the table. It came typed on a greeting card, one that would be sent from lover to lover, and accompanying it was a red rose tied on with green lace.

"What the fuck is this?" Longwell questioned. He looked up to ask the waitress if she knew who'd delivered the message, but she was already gone. He opened the incognito card and began to read.

The meeting place has been decided. You may know it when you find it, but then again you may not. When you're there, hit the swimming hole if you want. A river runs through the back, and a dip-in may bring you the serene drip that you're really looking for. River water carries away any toxin, any reek, it unties knots. The colder the water – the better. The meeting point is not the river. The river runs behind the hilltop. In the woods. The hilltop is the meeting point. You can't miss it. It's a perfect half-moon. If you're trying to find some sort of meaning in that, its shape that is, I think you'll be pleasantly surprised. There's no significance to it that isn't already apparent. No meaning that couldn't be reached with a hacksaw, written in your daily wordcross, or littered in the salt on your potato skins. I suppose specific directions should be given to ensure you find this exact location. The directions are as follows: ask yourself why the chicken crossed the road and in the company of whom. Next consider why the most contagious of all ailments is clearly the yawn. And then proceed to mix together paints in the colors blue, yellow, red, and orange. A good look into the color blend combined with consideration of these teases will lead you unquestionably to this hilltop. If it doesn't, you can get there by driving north up Highway 56, after you cross the train tracks take a left onto the dirt road, down there you'll see a grey barn on your right, park your car at the road's end, and you'll see the hill behind the barn. The other party will meet you at the top, 2:00 pm, for the hand-off.

"What the fuck is this?" he asked again.

Page dotted the last line of his note. He laughed to himself and folded it shut. In short flicks of the wrist, he struck the end of his pen against the wall of Harold's Store while staring into its bricks. The note got tucked down into his pocket, and he turned to face the alley wind. He held his jacket closed by sticking his hands in the front pockets and crossing his arms at the wrist, not by the zip. A lamppost hooked into the street at the alley's end, its light spread over the night dimly. Page headed towards it. People mingled on the sidewalk, and strolled freely down the barely lit road. Some in groups, others alone – puffing out smoke or just their breath into the cool night. Page caught the cold as he emerged back onto the sidewalk. A chilly wind moved under his nose and made him quiver.

"Page, right?" inquired a passing man.

"Yeah." He sniffed.

"Oh, I was just in the Fish Kettle," the man said pointing to its door, just beyond them.

"Oh yeah?" Page asked as if he didn't care.

The man's just rougher than five o'clock shadow had been neatly cropped above his neck and had yet to bristle his overweight cheeks. "Yeah," he said back softly. His hair curled up in a placed mess and was fastened in gel. "Anyways, your friend is in there looking for you. He's in there yelling. Being an obnoxious fuck," the man said and walked on.

A bit bewildered though not surprised, Page took the few steps between him and the Fish Kettle's door.

"There he is! Page!" Longwell shouted standing up from his seat. Staggering a bit, he opened up his arms. "I told you he'd be coming," he yelled back to nobody in particular. "Come here, give me a hug."

Page walked over. The bar's heat allowed him to open his jacket, and the yellow lighting eased off the heather green walls. Page hugged Longwell and laughed. "What's the occasion?"

"The occasion?" Longwell said pointing back at him. "Well my friend the occasion is us getting some well-deserved money. A little greenback to put between us and the Man. No more grinding on your leather ass, huh?"

"What are you talking about?"

"I got a note from ahh – the mob guys. Said we're all set," Longwell swallowed hard. "The deal's happening, an easy hand off." He pretended to be a quarterback and acted as if he was handing a football off to Page.

"Oh, really?" Page responded, taking the handoff to his stomach but not moving.

"Yeah, you're still in right?" He asked as if

implying the answer would of course be 'yes'.

"Yeah, man. I'm in," Page said patting Longwell's shoulder and looking around the room.

"Alright," Longwell nodded while eyeing Page. "You all right?"

"Yeah, what do you mean? I feel great. How about a drink?"

"Alright, now we're talking," Longwell said and lightly hit Page's arm while turning away from him. He looked over to Colander already sitting at the table. "He's fine."

"Give the people what they wanna see, huh?" Page laughed. "Give me a little bit of that somethin' and I'll entertain ya."

Longwell began to laugh quite well though silent. He let some cackle out. "You wanna hear a fucking story?" he said, acting as if he were the one drunk, obnoxious, and ready to entertain. This was an easy role for him to play. "I'll tell you a fuckin' story."

"Yeah!" Page said laughing. "That's all it takes. Just a little somethin'. Otherwise, man, I'm just gonna be a bump on your log."

"Log your bump," Slark said quickly.

"Log my – " Colander began thinking. "Oh, bump," he laughed. "Yes, log it," he flicked his wrist in the air as if he were making a checkmark.

Longwell began to laugh again. His mouth gaped open and his short pointed nose scrunched. He looked like a feather-plucked owl.

The Fish Kettle was packed full that night. Standing patrons clogged up the walkways between the booths, the round tables, and chairs. To get to the barfront, one pushed through shoulder to shoulder, patting the backs of those they had disturbed. Page and his friends sat at a round table in the very back. Each sitting in their own chair, leaning on un-cushioned armrests, and moving drinks from their mouths to the table – the waitress checked back often. A clamor held the air, though some voices separated and individual shouts shot above the room's noise.

"So I woke up this morning naked," Springler offered to the table.

"Do you generally sleep in the nude?" Colander asked.

"No," Springler answered dismissingly.

"I assume there was a lady involved then," Longwell said.

"Yeah – well, sort of. When I woke up, there wasn't anyone else there," he laughed and rested his palms on the top of his head as he leaned back. "Smitty, the kid who lives downstairs, calls me up in the morning, says my clothes are scattered all over his living room floor."

Everyone began to laugh.

"What? I think we need the whole story to go with that," Page demanded.

"Yeah, alright," Springler started as if bothered, but couldn't keep his face straight for too long. "So I'm trying to bang this girl – a good looking one too, you know, nice ass, nice tits, nice everything. And I must have been spitting mad game 'cus this girl was buying it –"

"Hey don't sell yourself short, you get some

hot chicks," Page affirmed. "I think it's your incoherent screaming that finally reels 'em in."

"No – I know – that's true," he agreed, smiling. "Alright, so it may not have been possible for this girl to even understand what I was saying, but she was coming on to me big time. I could tell she wanted to touch me."

The table laughed again.

Colander said, "Right."

"But I really have no idea what happened. I was blacked out. Woo – gone," he cut his hand through the air. "I remember talking to her, she had her elbow on my knee and was like resting her head in her hand, and we were talking and everything, god knows what about, and then next thing I remember, I'm waking up in my bed, alone and naked. My clothes nowhere to be seen," he began to laugh and took a sip of his drink. "They were downstairs at Smitty's place, right? So that means I walked up two flights of stairs, from Smitty's, buck-ass naked."

"With that fat ass? You coulda given the old lady on your floor another heart attack," Slark said snickering.

"And I remember none of this," Springler said cutting the air with his hand again. "I hope I boned her," he said a little quieter, rubbing his chin.

All at the table ate up each other's wallow. There was no tip-toeing around the truth, and the more embarrassing the story the better. In later conversations, a prior incident may be brought up to further the ribbing, but it was always done in good fun, without malice, and with no other intention but to prolong the entertainment. Nobody was spared, so nobody was hurt. It came about in an almost therapeutic way. Tough skin mandatory, but it let you know who your friends were, and the relief of your personal grievances aired, your troubles known, and your haunting stories told, kept your money to yourself and out of the practice of psychiatry.

"Hey, can we get him another drink here?" Longwell called to the waitress. He looked at Springler happily. "He got laid last night, let's assume it."

"I can feel it in my bones," Springler said, pointing to it as evidence.

When the Fish Kettle was set to close, Longwell, Page, and Colander were the only ones left at the table.

Page sipped his drink in-between some of his words. "They always think people kill themselves for a reason. But that can't always be true. Maybe sometimes. But other times they must kill themselves because they don't have anymore reasons. That's a choice they make, a final one, and I think the survivors don't have much place in not being fine with that. You can't take death so personal. We have to understand that if someone feels they don't want to face this life anymore, then they have all the reason in the world to let go and set sail for some unknown," Page stopped and thought about his words. "Like Magellan."

"Magellan?" Longwell asked, hardly believing what he heard.

"Sailed to the unknown world. For all he knew, he coulda fallen off the world's edge."

"You're fucking crazy," Longwell told him. "A real sensitive prick too. Why the hell are you talking about killing yourself anyways? Where did that come from?"

"I'm not talking about really killing myself. I'm just talking about killing yourself," Page paused. "I don't know why it came to my mind. It just came."

"Wouldn't the lack of a reason to live be a reason that they did kill themselves?" Colander asked.

"Alright, shut up. Listen," Longwell interrupted. He became real business-like, and said, "So this note, it's got this bunch of horseshit, but says we gotta meet some other guys at the top of some hill. That's where the deal goes. There's a hand off, 2:00 pm the day they had told us before. What? That's a week from now?"

"Yeah," Colander said.

"Alright, a week," Longwell said decisively. "That's not bad. I can go another week on what I got. Page, you're fine. Colander, if you ever need anything, you ask us."

Colander nodded. "A fork was stolen from my place today," he told them.

Longwell gave a skeptical look. "A fork?"

"Yeah, right from my kitchen table."

Longwell looked at Page. "Who goes around stealing forks?" Longwell asked.

"I don't know," Colander answered defensively. "Someone's been messing around my building though. Remember that night I told you I got followed home."

The other two struggled to remember.

"And then this morning someone broke into the building and was fooling around with the smoke detector on my floor. The superintendent sees him and starts yelling. I go out to see what the commotion is, musta left my door open, because I come back in and my fork is missing, the syrup's been spilled, and my window's open."

"Did they ever catch the guy?" Page asked.

"No. But I'll tell you, the cop who came and checked out the smoke alarm, he seemed real suspicious."

"You think the cops are stealing your forks?" Longwell sarcastically asked.

"I don't know who is stealing my forks. I know the cop who said the guy stole only batteries from the smoke alarm was full of shit though."

The last couple in the Kettle picked-up their coats and put them on. The man fastened her buttons and she happily waited, the top of her head coming up to his chin. Young hair fell along her neck, and her gaze ranged over to the only other three men in the place. She caught Page looking at her. As the man reached her last button, without breaking Page's eyes, she kissed the man's cheek. He took her by the hand, the couple exited, and left was only the three of them.

"Well," Longwell offered before gulping the bottom of his cup, "I suppose that's it for me." He stood up from the table and put his jacket on. "Stolen forks, stolen AA batteries. Whew. It's a high stakes world out there. Sounds like you got a real case on your hands there, Sherlock," he said to Colander.

"Yes I do," Colander said finishing his drink and standing up a bit wobbly.

"All the sinners, saints," Page remarked, drunkenly aloof.

The next evening, Colander and Longwell were standing with Page in his kitchen. Colander leaned back against the counter, and watched Page pace from the refrigerator to a window at the kitchen's edge. Longwell was inspecting his fingernails, while keeping an eye on the TV.

"Past two nights, all the dinner I've had is cereal," Page said.

"Real healthy," Colander replied.

"Well it has been Wheaties." He stopped to smile.

Longwell laughed. "So you've been keeping strong."

"I'm outta milk though."

"Use orange juice," Colander suggested. "It's surprisingly good."

"That's gross. Alright, fuck dinner. I'm not hungry anyways. We gotta go meet up with Addie and get to this party."

Longwell announced, "Alright, party time, ba-beh!" And the three started for the door. "Do you like that? Ba-beh! Does that sound cool?" he asked.

Colander opened the door for Page and stood beside it, "No, I don't," he told him. "It sounds terrible."

"What the fuck do you know?" Longwell asked, and then followed Page out the door.

The Lady of Huntington Street's real name was Giselle. Freshly settled with a man, she got pregnant, had the kid, freaked, split, left it for the husband, and moved to the furthest end of Huntington Street. That was nearly a year ago. The pregnancy had done nothing to her figure. The baby plopped out, and she shrunk back down to her original size – her hourglass shape.

The entrance to her apartment was subterranean. A slight staircase descended from Huntington Street's sidewalk, its abrupt end finishing at giant double doors, and on their other side, another staircase dropped down even further into the foyer.

Shortly after the bell ringing, Giselle was standing in the open doorway. She eyed Addie, Colander and Longwell, and she smiled mischievously at Page. Golden shoulders rose above the white lace of her shirt, and her belly-button remained exposed as the shirt's bottom ended just above it. The low-cut pants she wore were tan, tied together at the top with a ribbon belt, and stretched tightly down her long legs. Page took his arm from Addie, and greeted Giselle with a hug. The woman's hair was neatly cut so as to brush on her bare shoulder. It too was golden, and Page's palm took a handful of it, cupping the back of her head as they embraced.

"I couldn't be happier to see you."

"Me?" Page acted surprised and put on a big smile.

"Yes, you! Where have you been?" Giselle asked, putting an arm around the small of his back.

"Oh, everywhere," he replied.

"Everywhere? Yeah, you? Right," she answered.

"Hey –" Page started, but was interrupted by Giselle encouraging everyone to come inside.

"Come now," she said. "There's nothing out there." She walked the group through the doorway and into the center of the foyer. "Well, this is my home."

In front of them were three identical horseshoe-shaped openings, the outer two arched the entrances of staircases going up into the house, while the middle, slight in depth, kept a wooden chest. The last step of either staircase fell-out from under the arch and into the foyer. The room's cylindrical shape combined with the cream marble brick of the walls and stairs created a prestige that emanated throughout the house.

"It's been too long since you last came – a week?" Giselle asked Page.

Page stuck both hands into his hair. "A week? No." He moved a hand onto his chin and tilted his head back. He got a view of the low hanging chandelier, the room's only light. "It has been too long though. How have you been?"

Colander had wandered over towards the middle cavern, and was inspecting the top of the chest with amusement. Green vines had been drawn along its border, and in the center of the top and bottom edge were giant suns.

"I'm great. Very good. I'm in happiness," she said presenting the inside of her house with her hands out. Her arms curled smooth and long.

"Of course," Page said glowing, and as if he already should have known.

"In happiness?" Addie asked.

Giselle smiled, oblivious to any sourness.

"Happiness," Longwell answered, pushing his way from behind Addie and up one of the staircases. Only a few steps in, the staircases connected on a landing, and then only one case went the rest of the way up.

The lone staircase climbed in a spin up the center of the house. Extra care had been taken during one of its restorations to ensure the ascent wouldn't be too steep or the spin too sharp. Along the stairwell was a thin railing, the walls remaining bare, and it was only the subtle imperfections of each marble brick that distinguished each from the other. Every step echoed – the reverberations providing the impression that one was living in a solemn world.

Longwell said to Colander, who was a couple steps behind him, "This place is like a castle."

"I know. I can't wait to get fucked up here,"

Colander replied.

Longwell held back laughter.

In front of them was Giselle leading the way, she was bringing along Page, whose one hand was raking against the walls and whose other was taken-up in Giselle's. In the rear, Addie quietly followed. She ascended the stairs, gripped by her own fascinations of the house, and moving in a young girl's naïve spell.

"Hey, Addie. Page looks pretty lonely up there, huh?" Longwell said turning around to her.

Colander was able to put the hold on his laughter.

She didn't respond, but gave Longwell a dirty though embarrassed look.

Longwell was somehow pleased with himself.

Already at the stairwell's top, Giselle and Page stood alone. Page looked at Giselle with boyish excitement. His hair waved brashly around, his knees unable to keep still while his shoulders bobbed. He smiled in at Giselle, and she watched him.

"What are you looking at?" he asked.

"Nothing," she replied nonchalantly, and began to lightly slap her hands against her thighs, averting her eyes.

Page nodded, turned his head, and peeked down the stairs.

While he wasn't looking, she kissed him quickly on the cheek, came out of it, and pretended to still have been staring off at the ceiling's far corner. The bottom of her hair swayed along her shoulders from the movement.

Page began to laugh and put his hand on his cheek. "Hey," he took a step towards her pointing.

"What?" she challenged seriously and moved her face close into his.

"I got an eye on you."

She didn't take her eyes off of his lips, and she made a kiss with her own.

Longwell and Colander just then came to the top of the stairs. Page took a step back. "I'm sorry, I don't think I've made proper introductions here," he said. "Giselle, these are two of my very good friends, Longwell and this is Colander."

"Oh, good. Yeah, Page, where are your manners? Come on guys." She motioned for Colander and Longwell to push forward with her. "As you know I'm Giselle, and again, welcome. I hope we'll have a good time."

"You have an awesome house," Colander blurted out as he caught up to her.

Page waited at the top of the stairs for Addie.

"Oh, thank you," Giselle replied. "I'm so glad you guys could all come. The party should be great. All the hits, the people, and the good favors," she smiled at the two of them as they walked beside her.

Longwell said, "Alright, ba-beh!"

Colander gave him a stern look and shook his head as if to say 'no'.

Longwell returned the look with one that recognized the error of his way.

The second floor had multiple hallways that led to different parts of the house. The three continued down one of them, Giselle leading the way and the conversation.

Page greeted Addie at the top of the stairs. "Pretty unreal, huh?"

"Hmmm, yeah," she dully replied.

Page could sense her attitude, but immediately ignored it. The two walked in the direction Giselle had taken Longwell and Colander, though they lagged far behind. The hallway they moved through was fairly narrow and lined with doors that were usually kept closed.

"This is a great place. Wonder how she got something like this," Page thought aloud.

"She's probably the type that gets anything she wants."

Page thought about that for a second and then said, "I'm always wanting things lately. I find the more I get though, the more I want something else. I've been a bit insatiable as of late," he said, and then discovered a hair on his tongue. He picked it off, and tried to flick it from his nail.

Addie didn't say anything, and she watched the ground go by under her.

"The party should be fun. Giselle said a lot of people are already here, and McGee, Springler, everyone's coming."

"That'll be nice."

"Yes."

Page walked the hallway in long steps. He would find himself a few strides ahead of Addie, and he'd turn back or sideways, fidgeting, hiding impatience, race scratching his fingers through his hair. At times, he'd study one of the room's wall hangings, its dribbling curtains, or ornamental empty boxes. Addie purposefully moved slow, and the hallway was long, a thin red runner carpet rolling the length of it as if to bring in royalty.

"Tony."

"Tony?"

"Tony!"

Three party-goers made it quickly down the hallway, two headed straight into the tiny room, and the third turned to shut the door behind them.

Page had backed up into the wall to avoid the rush.

McGee began talking again. "Like I was saying, you can't stare at that ass for too long. It's like the sun, man! You'll just freeze up. You're stuck and saying, 'I know of nothing else that exists but this woman's butt,'" McGee said dazing his eyes and staring forward.

Page's laughter bent him forward a little then he quickly came back for more banter, now going into McGee's ear. Page raised his hand to block any loose words.

McGee listened and the two laughed.

"And you know that's not the worst place for it to break off," McGee concluded, and the two laughed again.

"No shit, man," Page agreed fishing out a cigarette.

"Anyways, you better look out. Longwell's over there talking to Addie, you know how that gets. He's been especially *on* tonight too." McGee patted the top of Page's shoulder and walked away.

Page finished his drink with a deep swig, looked over at Longwell and Addie, saw them sitting amongst a group of other mutual friends, and then setout to find where Giselle had gone to.

"Hey, here's a dollar Addie, how bout you go get me another drink?" Longwell offered her.

"What? No," she said bothered.

"Yeah, come on. I don't want to have to get up. Take the dollar, go get me a drink and get yourself one too. It wouldn't hurt to put a smile on your face either. This is no funeral. Why don't you stop bringing everyone down?"

"I don't bring people down."

"Yeah, you're right. You are a bundle of joy. I know if I want to have a good time, I call you right up," Longwell joked and finished his beer with a tasty gulp. He shook the empty bottle in front of Addie to show it empty.

"No, I'm not getting you another drink."

"Come on. Two dollars," he offered. "Hey McGee, you going to get another drink?"

"Yeah," McGee answered.

"Bring me one, will you? I asked Addie, but the bitch is gonna charge me three dollars to do it."

"Yeah, I'll get you one," McGee replied.

"I only got two, lady!" Longwell leaned over and yelled towards Addie.

She didn't move.

McGee was quickly back.

"See, Addie. That is what human beings do for each other. We don't all just sit around and mope."

Page found Giselle in the midst of light conversation with a few others. He stayed safely distanced, but came into her view and called her attention through head nods, eye lifts, and smiles. She sent her own gestures, and in so signaled for him to meet her at the opening of the hallway across the room.

Page refilled his drink and waited for Giselle to excuse herself from the group. She did so politely, shining an apologetic smile at the women, and parallelizing the men with a touch on the arm. To a couple of guests on her way by, she said hello and played the role of gracious host, but once she saw Page standing alone at the hallway entrance she made her way much more swiftly.

She walked by him and said "Follow me," while dragging a finger in the air.

The hallway they walked through wrapped around the perimeter of the house, and Giselle hurried him down it, not too far, before they came to a single door that led out to her veranda. With him in the front, she put her hands around the back of his shoulders, thumbs at the base of his neck, her long fingers tapping down on the top of his chest, and she pushed him out the doorway.

Addie had left Longwell and the rest of the people she knew, and now smoked a cigarette with a few other women – all of which draped themselves in black – eye liner, clothes, and demeanor. One spoke no European language save English, but she talked like she did.

"Dese people here. I know none of them, yet they are all my friends," she said straight-faced, and with a slim cigarette in-between her fingers.

Addie nodded with her eyes lowered.

"And how do yuu know Ms. Giselle?" the same woman asked of Addie.

"Well, I don't know her. My boyfriend though, he – umm – he knows her."

"Oh," the woman replied slowly, and the rest of the women in the circle nodded, flashing their eyes elsewhere.

"She's a wonderful woman," another in the circle said. She wore black gloves that extended nearly to her elbow. The gloves were of the same translucent material that made up her knee-high stockings, indiscreetly patterned, and typical of any woman who would be generalized as a Goth. Her lipstick was nearly black too. "Giselle somehow has money and she donates to charities in need regularly, though I've never known her to work a day of her life," the woman said and then looked away.

"Giselle's a people person," the European accented woman continued. "She knows her way in the art of healing, and I've never known her to say anything mean about anyone."

The Goth took a drag of her cigarette and as the smoke rushed out, she said under her breath, "Just don't let her anywhere the hell near your man."

Page took a deep breath in up the nose. Released it, and came down shaking his arms. "Ooo," he said, giving Giselle a grin.

She bent over the railing next, took hers, and ran her finger above her lip. She turned to Page, and put her hands in his hair. "Now, we talk. Come. Sit."

Page brought one of the chairs across from another. They were outdoor patio seats, oversized and made of wood, but they leaned back at a comfortable angle. Beyond the veranda, the street was relatively quiet, as most were inside somewhere, in Giselle's house or elsewhere. The night was mild, but a chilly breeze would at times whip through. Page was properly dressed for the chill, while Giselle goosebumped.

"You look unhappy. Tired," she told him.

"I do?" Page's face glared his acknowledgment, but he acted as if he was surprised to hear that. "You're not the first person that's said that to me actually," Page admitted. He leaned forward to take a cigarette out.

"Well, it's plain to see. You are extra pale, and your eyes too closed," Giselle examined and then crossed her legs. She flicked up a flame in her lighter, and held it out to him.

"I've been in a vicious lull, so-to-speak."

"That sounds terrible," Giselle replied, taking her own cigarette out. "You know what I do when I lull?"

"I didn't know you did lull."

She briefly looked away, put her lower lip over the top and shrugged. "We all lull."

In agreement, Page shrugged back.

Longwell spotted Addie standing in the group she'd latched to, and he knew exactly where Page was.

"Hey, Addie. Have you seen Page?" he asked while seated on the arm of a couch. He nearly fell when he tried to cross his legs, he caught his balance and then hiccupped.

Addie pretended like she didn't hear him.

"Hey, I'm looking for Page. Has anyone seen him?" he called out to the entire room. "No? Oh, ok. I'll keep an eye out for the guy who is running from hell as fast as he can, shouting 'heaven!', and trying to unbuckle his pants at the same time," a smirk came onto Longwell's face, but he quickly covered it. "Yeah, there's a good chance that'd be Page."

Drunk on abuse, Addie turned to her ladies, "Excuse me," she said.

Colander and McGee anticipated anxiously as the insulted woman stalwartly marched towards Longwell. She didn't move her eyes off of him.

"Uh-oh," Longwell joked. "It's Satan herself."

Colander and McGee didn't dare laugh.

Addie took a last drag off her cigarette as she approached the couch's arm. A quick turn of the wrist, and she drove the cigarette down through Longwell's pant-leg and put it out on the skin of his knee. "Go fuck yourself," she simply said.

Longwell yelled out in pain. "You bitch!"

Colander smacked his hand against his mouth to keep back the laughter.

McGee stayed straight-faced.

And Addie turned, heading for the room's exit. Half-way there the tears came, and she began to run.

"When I lull," Giselle lowered her gaze at Page. Setting her cigarette down, she crawled up into his chair and spoke slowly.

Page dropped his cigarette too.

"I find someone who I know to have an unlimited source of energy – a real all-nighter you know, someone who," her fingers traced from the corners of Page's eyes to his nose, and then down along the top of his cheekbone. She hovered face-to-face with him and continued, "knows where to lay their fingers," she spread her hands along the back of his neck, pushed in, and ran them all the way to his chest, "or where to wrap their legs," she began to laugh and dropped herself onto him.

"That sounds like a – ahh – a great cure for the lulls," Page said, putting his arms around her back – pulling her in.

"Anytime you want, baby," she said bringing her head out from the nape of his neck, and brushing her lips against his ear.

He gripped her by her bare stomach. "Later. We gotta get back to this party. We can't be gone for too long."

"Don't tease," she said bending back off him, her hands in her hair.

"No, really. I gotta get back in there. Addie's here. I have to put my boyfriend face back on," Page remarked, trying not to laugh.

Giselle came back in close to his face and draped her hair over his head. "You are right. Go see her. I get you later though." She gave him a kiss on the forehead, and then climbed off.

Page stood and straightened his shirt up. He sniffed and ran a finger over his cheek, while Giselle moved the chairs back.

"Hey, let's do one more – hmm?" Page propositioned her, raising his nose.

"Oh, I do like you," she said aloud to herself.

"You know you put Page into some real shit with what you just pulled with Addie, right?" McGee asked of Longwell.

"What are you talking about? I'm the one who got physically assaulted."

"He's going to now have to deal with all the flack she's gonna give him for you being an ass."

"Are you kidding? Fuck him. Where is he right now? Off with gorgeous perfect Giselle," Longwell said her name and raised a hand in the air. "Probably got his balls throat deep in her. If he really cared I think he'd be here, consoling his over-sensitive girlfriend, and saving her from guys," Longwell hiccupped again. "Fucking hiccups – guys like me who can't help but tell the truth."

"You're a real prick, Longwell," McGee said shaking his head and walking away.

Longwell looked to Colander, who was sitting on the couch with some other party-goers, his fingers dancing on his knee. "Bunch of big cry babies," Longwell said walking over to him.

"What?" Colander asked. He began slapping his knee.

"Nothing."

Page came through the hallway entrance and back into the room.

"Oh, look what the cat dragged in," said Longwell.

By the way his friends were looking at him, Page couldn't keep the smile off his face.

"What?" he asked.

"Nothing," Colander replied, looking him over. "How was it?"

"Fresh air? Good. Tony? Great."

Purposefully lagging behind, Giselle emerged next from the hallway, moving giddily and fixing her hair.

"You sly dog," Colander said shaking his head.

"Where's Addie?" Page asked, brushing off Colander's remark.

"She left," McGee told him.

"She what?"

"You smell like perfume," Colander told him.

"Gone, Longwell drove her out," McGee said nodding his head in Longwell's direction. "But not before she put her mark on the whole thing, I'd say."

"What you been up to buddy?" Page asked Longwell. He saw the burn mark in his jeans. "Cigarette fall out your mouth?"

"Hey, you better watch out for what she's gonna do to you," Longwell replied.

Page looked him in the eye and said nothing.

"I was just trying to have a good time," Longwell said defending himself.

Page nodded, his knees bouncing. "Did she say where she was going?"

"Nope, just ran out," McGee answered.

Page nodded again and looked over the room packed full of people. "Ok, well," he decided slowly, "anyone need a drink?"

The rest of the night passed in this general fashion, and under the pretense of the following sentiments and quotes:

Forgive me father, for I know not what I've done, what I'm doing, or – other things too – I'm sorry, I can't say that without laughing. Sometimes you need drugs to enjoy your sobriety. What's sober if you're never drunk? If you play your cards right, well I'm pretty easy, you do got cards, right? I know I had a beer. She's a fox. I'm a fox. So do you think that I could get some of whatever it is you got. People have been saying that? People are dumb. Scotch and ice will be all. What about lesbian porn? Nothing? Nothing. Oh, you don't know what you're missing. I spilled, oh don't worry it's just on myself. Oh where, oh where has my little friend Tony gone? Oh where, oh where could he be? No jokes, I'm telling it like it is now. What's funny, honey? It's gonna be nasty boogers in the morning. You eat organic? Oh, you're so lucky, you're gonna live to be, his speech paused and he began to giggle. Ninety-five!

Wohoo! Hook is the one who has it right, 'Death is the *only* adventure'. Peter just doesn't know yet. Oh man, I could go all night. Hey, fuck you.

And the night generally passed.

Page's bread popped out of the toaster golden brown. He yawned loudly, and his eyes were still only half-open. Leaning back at the torso, he yawned again.

"I never yawn twice," he started to say before the second yawn had fully come out.

Addie sat at the table with her head rested on her arm. She didn't look up, and pushed the fried egg around her plate.

"What? You want salt?" Page asked as he noticed her disinterest in the eggs he'd made her.

"Nope, plenty of salt."

Page eyed her suspiciously while sitting down at the table. He took a bite of bacon before buttering his toast.

Addie poked the egg's yellow center with her fork, and the warm yoke drained out. She still hadn't taken a bite.

Page looked around the kitchen blankly before asking, "What's the matter?"

"What's the matter? Did you even notice that I left *Giselle's* house?"

"What are you talking about? Of course I did."

"I left at not even eleven. Crying. Balling my

eyes out. I couldn't find you, and I ran the whole way back here. You didn't even come after me," she broke down and began crying.

"Addie, I didn't know where you went. And what was it that happened anyways? What were you crying over?"

"Longwell! He's such an asshole. He was so mean to me."

"Hey, come on Addie. Longwell's an ass to everybody. You can't let him bother you."

"And you, you didn't get back here until 4:30. And even by then, I could feel your legs still jittering around in the bed," she said accusing with a hand gesture in Page's direction.

Page let out a loud breath and looked over to his right.

"Of course you have nothing to say – you never do. And this *Giselle* girl, since when have you known her so well?"

Page took a bite of toast to get something in his mouth. "I just, ahh," he started, trying not to sound defensive, but he waited to finish until his food was chewed. "I, ahhh, she's just somebody I know," he said raising his voice. "I met her on the street."

"Yeah, I'll bet you know her. And it's great that you're going around meeting women on the streets," Addie quipped back.

"Hey! Where do you get off with an accusation like that?"

"Hardly just an accusation. I saw her with her arm around your back the whole time as we walked in. God knows where you were when I ran outta there. And all of you, you stare at her all googly-eyed," Addie said stabbing her eggs again. "*Oh, I live in happiness*," she mocked. "Well, why don't you take that happiness and go shove it up your ass."

"Now you're gonna bring her down for being happy? Well, sorry, but there are some people in this world that don't go around all the time acting down and glum."

"Are you throwing this back on me? As if this is my fault somehow?"

"It's nobody's fault. There is no fault," Page said with his hands out.

Addie didn't budge.

"Maybe Longwell has some fault. But even he, he's just constantly obnoxious. He can't help that."

"I don't ever want to see him again," Addie said trying to hold back more tears.

"Fine don't," Page dropped his toast on the plate. "But you're not telling me who I can hang out with. If you don't wanna see him, that's fine. You don't have to. I'll say something to him about talking to you like that too, but I choose my own friends," Page said pointing at himself. "And, I'm sorry, but I don't accept other people's input in that matter."

"Hangout with whoever you want. I don't care. But you sure can tell a lot about someone by the company they keep," is all she said.

"Yeah? What does that say about you?"

She didn't say anything back.

Page took a bite of his eggs and looked up at the ceiling. Addie's body was hung over the table. Under her worn grey t-shirt, her shoulders hunched. She kept her head up with weak hands against a trembling chin, a tear ran the length of her cheek, and into her eggs she began to sob.

Page looked back over at her, he said, "What the fuck is the matter with you now?"

She began weeping harder and covered her face, knocking the fork onto the floor with her elbow.

"Ok, Ok," Page said genuinely apologetic. He went over to her side of the table. "What's wrong, darling?" he asked moving her hands from her face. He tried to ease her head onto his shoulder, but she calmed, backed off, and locked eyes with him for a second.

Page waited cautiously.

She sniffed the snot back up her nose. "I don't want to be around anyone right now," she said softly, and then drifted her eyes off of him.

Page took it fairly well. "Yeah? Well, ok." He nodded a couple of times, stood up, and took a few steps to the side. "If you wanna go, go."

Colander too had not gotten home until very late. He didn't even try to sleep during the night, instead he waited until a ten a.m. crash to go to bed. When he woke up, the sun was already beginning to come down, and he had two missed calls from his mother. Leaning against his kitchen's counter, he called her back, and now listened impatiently to what she was saying.

"Mom, alright, but Mom – " Colander listened. "Yeah, but Ma – " he was cut-off again and made a face of anguish.

"Fine. Fine. Yes. Alright. I'll do it. Anyways. I got a job the other day, so I should be getting some money soon."

He'd been saving that for when he really needed it.

"No, it's not permanent. It's more like a one-time thing, but it's gonna pay well. I'm just working on one single job. What? Yeah, sorta- like construction."

On Colander's side of the line there were two distinct clicking sounds. He noticed them but said nothing.

"Well at this point, money is money right? It's not like I'm doing something – ahh – ahh, illegal."

There were two more distinct clicks.

"Are you clicking? Do you hear that clicking?"

When she said she heard nothing, Colander became alarmed and again suspicious.

"I gotta go, Mom," he said slowly. "Alright, I love you too."

After hanging up his phone, he went to the window, divided the shades, and peeked out onto the street. A couple of troublesome kids were outside throwing rocks at the telephone lines, but there was nobody else around. Colander looked back at the cell phone in his hand, its antenna extended.

"Well, what the fuck?" he said defeated and walked out of his kitchen.

That night was spent just as many of the others were. Binge amusements and forgetting. By the end, Longwell was in no shape to do anything but crash. Page picked up the tab, dragged his friend out and back to his place. He threw Longwell down onto the tiny couch, and then put himself to bed.

Page stopped typing when he heard rustling in the bedroom. He looked down into his coffee mug, and saw a thin layer of liquid left. He took a sip, but it was cold. Longwell came into the room yawning. Walking slowly and in the same pants he had worn the night before, he waddled back to the couch, dropped himself down onto it, and picked up the remote. Page turned from his desk chair to face him. He'd yet to mention anything about Addie.

"How'd you sleep?" Page asked.

"Terribly on this couch, I got a couple hours in the bed though."

Once Page couldn't sleep anymore, he'd let Longwell sleep in the bed while he got his day started. The few hours of sleep Longwell got on the bed were his only.

"Why the hell were you up so early?"

"Early? I got up at like one."

"Shit," Longwell said surprised. "What time is it now?"

"4:30."

"Oh God." Longwell rubbed his eyes.

"Well, you gotta start the day at some point," Page said extra chipper.

Longwell laughed loudly and broke out coughing. "I guess so," he said in a near choke.

Page got up and poured himself another cup of coffee. He asked Longwell if he wanted one, but he said he didn't.

"My stomach," he complained.

Page came back and sat in the living room chair. The two began laughing about the antics of the night before.

"How did I get this all over my shirt? And, what is it? It smells like –"

"It's guac," Page told him.

"Guacamole. I ate guacamole?"

Page laughed and sipped his coffee. "We all did. Colander ordered it." He put the mug down on the table and stared at it for a second. "Hey, so about this thing with the mob guy."

Longwell looked up at him, still in a state of just-awoken bewilderment.

Page continued. "Why the hell is he asking us to do the job? Why not one of his own guys?"

"I know. I thought of the same thing," Longwell paused, shuffling his hair back into place. "All I can figure is that he doesn't want to have any affiliation with it. They do this all the time. Use outside guys to do deals. That way, if things go bad, guys get caught or whatever, it doesn't get tied back to them."

"Well then does that make this a high-risk job?"

"High-risk? Come on. It's a hand-off at the top of some hill out in the country. We won't be there any more than thirty seconds. Really Page, this is easy money. You know, I'm just trying to get you a buck here. I wouldn't put us in harms way. He said we need three guys, that's how he wants it. If I just gotta hand some dude something, or have him hand me something, shit, even if it's not for the full $50,000. I'd take a couple kinky slaps on the ass as payment for doing that."

Page almost laughed then picked his coffee back up. "Well, alright man. Sounds good. It still makes me a bit nervous though, but with no risk comes no reward, huh?"

"Yeah baby, easy money."

"How many days we got?"

"Four. And hey that reminds me, you think we can take Addie's car?"

"Addie's car?" Page thought for a moment. "Yeah, I could ask her."

"Don't tell her it has anything to do with me though. That girl bitches at me non-stop. What the fuck's with her anyways?"

"She just ahhh – "

"She hammers nails into coffins."

Page tried to ignore him.

"I can't get a sentence out without her judging it with some holier than God bullshit."

"Alright easy," Page responded and wiped his eyes. "I told you, give her a break."

"Speaking of God, I saw a sign at some church a couple streets down, said they're having a pancake breakfast today. We could go get fed," Longwell suggested.

"Us? Man, I'm not going to some church to eat their pancakes," Page dismissed. "Plus it's five o'clock almost. They aren't pumping out pancakes all day." Page was quiet for a moment. He slouched lower into the recliner. "I need a girl who's gonna pump me out pancakes all day."

Longwell laughed.

"Need to get me one of them and *use* her," Page said looking off. "One that's got a soft ample breast," he said in a romantic voice. "Who doesn't like cuddly things?"

Longwell laughed harder. "Oh, breasts," he said as if starting an ode.

"It's their sixth sense."

"Tits are a sense?"

Page laughed and rubbed his finger over his eyes. "No man," he stopped and giggled, "They just have a sixth sense. Well, maybe it must be our sixth sense, not theirs. I'm not sure. But they don't even know it! Don't know they got it! Some do. But shit, the right girl, just let me fall asleep curled up next to you, you know, just let me bury my face in you. She could get whatever she wants out of me. I'm just a note ready to be rung. I got the pancake mix made, baby. I just need your heat."

"Feed the man his pancakes!" Longwell shouted.

"Aww – and I'm hungry."

The early evening passed, the sun with it. Longwell and Page hardly stood up during the time. In a conversational equilateral triangle with the television, talk on all sides continued. At one point, Longwell got up without saying a word, dropped his pants and settled back down into the couch with just boxers on. From the chair, Page questioned with a look.

"I'm hot," is all he replied. "You know, I don't even know if I feel like drinking tonight. I'm considering going back to bed for the next day or so."

"Oh, yeah? How come?"

"I don't know. It's these stomach problems," he said rubbing his robust belly. "Plus, I mean last night. You saw me."

"Yeah, you were in rare form," Page said while lighting a cigarette.

Longwell laughed. "Well, what can I say? I'm a great performer."

Page shrugged and blew out smoke.

The television went through a couple commercials.

"I don't know why I even said that. We both know I'll be pissing and throwing up all over myself by about ten o'clock tonight."

"Ha!" Page let out and then sighed.

"So how do you know that Giselle girl from the other night?" Longwell asked very all of a sudden.

Startled by his friend's question, Page took a moment to think it over.

"Giselle?"

"Yeah, the goddess living in her mansion."

"Right. Well, I got to know her through a certain sort of chance encounter," he paused. "I'd been walking down the, on the, west end – and I saw across the street from me this little puppy. You know, he's plugging along, pulling his owner by the leash, a Chocolate Lab puppy, and he's just got this tenacious zeal, this real thirst for what's out there, you know? It was great. I was having a moment to myself," Page put his palms on his chest.

Longwell listened with a short supply of patience.

"Unbeknownst to me, I was standing right in front of Giselle's house. I'd settled right underneath her – she was hanging off her veranda, directly above. All of a sudden, I notice these little things falling down all around me. I bend over and pick one up, and see that they're flower pedals. I look up and there's Giselle leaning down above me. Peering down at me, lookin' like an angel, man. You know, you've seen her. She's golden, that face and with her up there on the porch, she had this whole majesty about her. Like I'm bowing down to the sun. So I call up to her, 'hey, what are you doing up there? You're killing that flower. Picking it dead, limb by limb.' You know. 'Don't ya know?' I call up to her," Page began to laugh as he'd put his hand to his mouth as if to shout. "And she says back to me, 'Picking it limb by limb? Honey, I already tore it out by the roots – right from out the ground.' And she makes this gnarly sort of face."

Longwell smiled skeptically. "What the hell does that mean? Tore it out by the roots?"

"What the hell does that mean? It means that this girl – this woman – she is a soul eater!" Page yelled laughing.

Longwell understood and began to laugh too. "She'll bite right through your chest and devour your very soul. It's a terrible habit really. She lacks any manners."

"Exactly, man. And who's going to stop her? Who's going to not let her?" Page looked out the window. "Not me."

Longwell shook his head in agreement. He asked, "So did you go inside then?"

"Inside? No – hell no, man – she's a killer," he responded and fell back into the chair smiling. "I went over and pet the puppy."

"You're such a bullshiter," Longwell said laughing. "I mean, do you ever really say anything? You're either talking a million miles an hour about nothing or not saying half-a-shit."

Page began to laugh.

"You know for somebody who acts as if they sure do deserve everything in the world, you really don't do anything for it. You're a moper. You mope. Addie does too. It's a wonder you guys even got up and found each other."

"What can I say?" Page asked with a big smile. "I'm a man of my time."

"A fucked up time, man. I don't know whether to show my face or just keep my drunken self to my-drunken-self. That's why Huntington Street is nice. I like the feeling of seclusion it has. I may get a place here after this whole deal goes down, once I have some more money."

"Oh yeah?"

"Yeah," Longwell said turning back to the TV. "Hey, check out this knife I bought," he said walking over to his bag, and pulling it out unsheathed.

"Where'd you get that?"

"That store next to the Fish Kettle. Harold's Store of All Things, it's called."

"Oh yeah, I know it."

"Yeah," Longwell said. He made a couple stabbing motions into the air, and then sat back down with it.

"What do you need that for?"

"Nothing really," he replied quickly and threw the knife down onto the end table. "Just for play," he said in a childish manner.

"Well," Page said standing up, "I'm outta coffee. You wanna go down to the Kettle?" Page asked.

"Yeah, sure."

"I'll call Colander."

The front room of the Fish Kettle had one table that extended further out onto the sidewalk than any of the rest. The table sat on a platform, which had been built to impose a solitude that wasn't really there. In-between the table and the sidewalk was a window with three glass panes segmented into equal rectangles. The three friends sat at this table and had been passing their time in silence mostly – idly watching the people pass.

"Oh, look. McGee's coming down the sidewalk," Colander noticed. He pointed out the window, towards the north, and in the direction McGee walked from.

"Big Balls McGee," Longwell said deepening his voice and putting a hand over his mouth. "He's a school-boy bitch."

"I'm going to get him," Colander announced. He got out of his chair, and undid his belt at the same time. "Knock on the window when he gets right in front of it," he told Page.

Page responded with a snicker of anticipation. Once Colander was ready, and McGee was directly passing, he knocked hard twice on the window.

Coming down the street, McGee had passed

all the storefronts without taking a notice of them, moving obliviously until hearing the knocks. He turned his head to see what the banging was about just as Colander's bare ass pressed into a suction against the window.

"Oh, god!" McGee looked on in wide-eyed horror before taking a step back. Upon seeing Page and Longwell sitting on the other side of the window and Colander's wonderfully proud face, McGee bent over at the waist, and soon was on all fours heaving the laughter.

A few on-lookers passed. They paused for a moment in half amusement and wondered about the unquestionable absurdity of such a scene's backstory, a young man down on all fours, alone in the middle of the sidewalk, laughing hysterically, quickly though they moved on with their day. Colander had buttoned his pants back up, satisfied. Page had his hands pressed against his eyes, tears leaking down his cheeks in delighted disgust, face red, and his shoulders bouncing. McGee rolled over onto his back right there on the sidewalk, gasping breaths in-between laughter spasms.

In a cold office building, a young journalist, an interviewer, tapped his pencil to break the drone of the air conditioning. He struck an idea. The newspaper would write a string of articles with the intention of renewing its readers' interest in the day's faded stars. A where- are-they-now sort of ploy. The editor sprung for it, calling the idea, "a gesture of goodwill to those fallen off course. After all," he delighted, "in life, at times it takes only the tiniest little nudge on the backside to get someone started-up again." His understudy, Oktavio, the interviewer, insisted upon leading the assignment. With his wish granted, he thumbed through his mind's pages of the washed out, the once known, once recognized, and once publicized.

Page was sitting alone on his couch around ten in the morning. His hair still had the rub of his sleep in it, and he'd woken up tired. The phone rang and he watched it for a moment before answering it. He listened with a straight look and his mouth shut. He said, "You wanna ask me about what?"

By one in the afternoon, the Fish Kettle had only a few early-birds inside. Page sat at one end of a table with his hat on and shirt tucked in. He had ordered a coffee and lightly sipped it in-between cigarette smoke. He stared at the empty chair across from him, biting his gums.

The interviewer walked onto Huntington Street from the east, and showed up at the Fish Kettle just when he said he was going to. As he came in, he wiped his shoes on a mat as the day was wet. A cold fall day where the drops were almost snow. He recognized Page immediately. There was a brief introduction and a few preliminary questions before the interview began.

Oktavio responded to Page with, "yeah, but you enjoyed some success. When you were fairly young too. Do you find your fame, even if it was minor, to ever get in the way of living your daily life?"

"Well yeah maybe before, but here, no, not really. Nobody recognizes me, and if they do, well they're not saying anything. I blend in with all the other – whatevers. I think my fame was only ten minutes."

The interviewer laughed. "Ten minutes? When's your other five coming?"

"I don't know," Page said slowly. "I'm not sure I want them. The last five often become the most notorious."

"Notorious? How so?"

"Well there's gotta be an ending there somehow. Once your fifteen minutes are up, you know, there's no sixteenth. There's some fall there coming. I mean, what are you gonna do then?"

"I don't know, settle down. Ease into your next life while leaning on the money your fame made you. Start a family maybe?"

"Oh," Page said as if he would bask in the idea. "That would be nice," he nodded.

"Not for you?"

"No, I think it could be for me". Page put his cigarette out. "It's just not that easy. It's complicated. Overwhelmingly. There is no clear path to it, you know? The only thing you really can know, that's clear-cut, and apparent is your exact moment. The thought you're just now having. I mean can you be sure about anything else? There's nothing else you can point your finger to as real and count on. So how do you go about your future? Things are false and true all at the same time. You make the decision and you don't know to rock your heels back and forth to it, or bury your head in the sand. Realities like that can weigh so much. But – " Page watched his finger trace a crack that ran through the table's end, "but to find ease and comfort in the world, you have to find the person who's going to make all those uncertain kind of thoughts go away – at least I do – someone who'll make me not remember anything like that anymore. I don't want to think about uncertainties. It's just not something I can do alone though."

Two girls at a table nearby broke into an obnoxious laughter, but Page's eyes didn't move. The interviewer scribbled a note without saying anything.

"You haven't found her yet?" Oktavio prodded.

"No man, I found her," Page replied quickly. "She's just disconnected her phone. Moved away. Had plastic surgery. Wears a wig now."

Oktavio was silent for a moment. He then began to laugh. "She took up and ran?"

"She must have." Page took a sip of coffee.

"Ok, well I found out you went to school for a number of years, what did you take away from that? What did you learn?"

"School?" Page incredulously replied. His eyes shot up to the ceiling. "Man, where did you hear that?" he asked leaning over the table.

"Little bit of research."

"Oh. Well, I'd say school taught me how to do things against my will. To do what others think, what they wanted me to do. That's really not all that useful anymore though."

"How come?"

"'Cus why would I wanna keep on doing that? I embrace my own will now. It's much nicer this way," he said leaning in again.

"Did you quit school?"

"Right away. Though I still was enrolled. I attended classes occasionally."

"Why'd you stay?"

"Well at the time, there was just nowhere else to go. Depending on where you came from, where you were brought up, you could be sucked-up into going on with school. At the same time though, school's not the worst thing. It gets in the way of anyone who has their own drive to," Page began to stumble, "drive to really educate themselves. You know, some people are only being crushed by sitting there in a chair all day in a classroom. The best thing school did was infuse in me the point that there was something else out there. It gave me a desire for anything else. It's a look into Alice's tunnel. Now if you wanna go to school, then that's fine, it's there for certain people, but at the same time you have to realize it isn't for everyone." Page smiled. "I did have fun at school though."

"What kind of fun? Partying and stuff, right?" Oktavio grinned.

"Oh – well yeah that's just how it goes. I mean, you know that," Page continued quickly and didn't allow the interviewer to question whether he actually did. "I made some good friends out there. You know, everyone was stuck in the same thing, looking for their own way out."

"Own way out of what?"

"Out of things like this."

"Like this?"

"Out of being constantly questioned, and having someone waiting for your answer, then they judge it, you know, put a little mark next to your name and try to get you worried about it."

Oktavio nodded. "Ok, what kind of friends

were they that you were making?"

"Man, any kind of friends you want. Come on."

"Well, what's the kind of friend that you look for, who's good for your company?" Okatvio challenged.

Page looked down at the Fish Kettle floor. A bottle cap, upside down, rested just at his foot. He kicked it out from under the table. "The friends I keep now are people who let me be. I tend to get a little neurotic, they know that, and they let me be. I like it, you know? I just like it that way."

"You like to act neurotic?"

"Well, now I don't think you understand what I mean by 'I like'."

"Ok, you –"

"I say 'I like' and that means me, Page, this body here in front of you. But this body is a combination of a couple things. There's *me* and I have no control over that. It's different from the me that is actually conscious and floating around in this world. You know, the conscious me is just trying to figure out what the hell's going on. The other *me* doesn't care. But what 'I like' is not something I can be completely blamed for. I is a combination of me and *me*. And they're blending a little further down than I can reach. You're following this right? Now I take complete responsibility for *me* too. Not admitting 'yes, that's *me*' is copping out, it's not the kind of thinking that's gonna get the world anywhere. But I can't help what I like! It's just what there is for me at the time. Something is making me think 'I like this'," Page cupped his hands together, open as if holding an object and he moved them to his left. "Not that," he said with a laugh and moved the same gesture to the right. Page went silent for the next moment. "I, ahh – yeah, so I do act a little neurotic sometimes."

"Would you say your friends are neurotics as well?" Oktavio asked.

"Yes."

Oktavio waited while Page stared at him. He struck his usual pose, propping himself up with his chin in his palm, anchoring his elbow into the table, and using the base of his fingers to block his lips. Oktavio understood and looked through his notes for the next question. Page took out another cigarette.

"I'm sorry, what was your first name again?" Page asked.

"Oktavio," his interviewer replied.

"Right, Oktavio," Page sat quiet for a second. "You should wear a hat," he pointed with the cigarette.

Oktavio laughed. "Why?"

"A man should wear a hat," he told him. "What is it they say?" He put the cigarette in his mouth. "You need a hat to hang your home?"

"I think you got the saying wrong," Oktavio replied smiling.

"Oh. Yeah. Ok, well what's your next question?" he asked then lit the cigarette.

Oktavio shuffled through his papers without much concentration. He digested. "Ok, yeah, next question." He read straight from his notes. "What kind of influences did you have? Or do you have?"

"Influences? Well those come from nearly anywhere really. I mean, sure, there are a couple people I could name –"

"Yeah, like who?"

"Who?" Page rubbed from his chin to the bottom of his lip. "Like maybe that guy over there," Page said nodding in the man's direction.

Oktavio turned quickly to see who it was. "That guy?" he asked pointing his head at him.

"Yeah, that guy. You don't recognize him?"

"No."

"Oh. He's in here everyday. I suppose that may mean I am too – but that guy, he comes in everyday with his newspaper under his arm, and a calculator and notepad in his other hand. Never seen him talk to anybody but the waitress, just keeps ordering tea, runs through the newspaper, frantically is punching numbers, and then writing things down," Page made a bewildered face. "So I walk over one day and ask him what it is he's doing, and he looks up at me real bothered. Real cold-like, you know? Covers up his notebook with his forearm as if he doesn't trust me. So I'm looking at him a little funny, when he says to me, 'Jesus would already be dead if he ever did come back. They'd have lynched him this time.'" Page dropped an eyebrow and waited for Oktavio's reaction. "Cryptic, huh? Now, I have no idea what the hell this guy's talking about, but – I sorta nod and go to sit-back down, not trying to think too much about it, when a couple minutes later, the guy comes over and puts a piece of paper in front of me, walks right out the door. So I take a sip of my drink, sorta look around to see if anyone else saw what just happened and it doesn't seem like anyone did, so I unfold the note. It says January 14th, 1976."

"What happened that day?"

"I have no idea. Haven't talked to him since."

"And this influences you?"

"Oh yeah. Well it's blind belief. You know, a great necessary evil. It's not perfect and its folly, its flaw, is glaringly obvious. But isn't it beautiful? It isn't justified nor rationalized, it's just there pushing. Just waiting there for you to make something exist. It can get you in so much trouble! But you can sit there and hold a cup of water with no bottom on it. You know, and is the water gonna fall out, or is it somehow staying in? I don't know – how hard do you believe?"

"The results can be good or bad," Oktavio added.

"Yeah." Page looked down in his lap and rubbed his thumbs on top of one another. "It's really what influence is. Another way of putting it. You believe whatever it is to be perfect, beautiful, right. There's nothing physical about being influenced by something, somebody's work, or whatever – just as there's nothing physical about full-heartedly believing in something that's not there. Both are completely abstract."

"I find myself passive throughout the whole process of being influenced."

"You have to be. You have very little to do with it. It's a stretch of your disbelief. Maybe in that way it is physical. You're like 'ahhh someone can really do that?'" Page said so pretending, and bringing his hands up to clutch his face.

Oktavio nodded enthusiastically and scribbled something down.

At the table nearby, the same girl and her friend began singing loudly – "sweat baby, sweat baby" – and danced their fists in the air. Oktavio turned his view off Page and watched the girls with amused curiosity.

"Those girls are funny," he said.

Page looked, saw the girls, and then turned back with a slight smile. "Hmmm," he nodded and flicked the bottom of his cup a few times. "Us humans are much too complicated when we want to be."

The two men became more at ease with each other. Page's previous worries of being pinned to the table under the fork prong had all but vanished. Young Oktavio's nerves had calmed, and they got off topic to try and salvage the conversation.

"Why don't you think dogs ever want to pet us back?" Page asked trying to keep his face straight.

He'd turned the interview around.

"Because they're selfish!"

"They know it feels good."

"They lick."

"Who wants to get licked – by a dog?"

"I heard it's just because they like the salt on your skin anyways," Oktavio said.

"Selfish bastards."

Oktavio laughed once. "Alright, gotta finish this."

"Ok, back to work, boss."

"So what about now? What is it you are doing now?"

"Umm." Page's head ducked down, and he stopped thinking. The momentary pause lasted. He reached for his hat on the table and straightened it on his head. Oktavio's eyes didn't leave him.

"Just trying to keep busy." Page said the word 'busy' slow and his focus was on the coffee cup. His finger traced along the handle of the teaspoon. He pushed his hat down further onto his head. "You know?"

"That's good," the interviewer responded, now a bit embarrassed.

Page looked back up at Oktavio. "It's healthy," he responded.

Page parted ways with Oktavio at the Fish Kettle's doors. A goodbye, a wave, and he never saw him again. Page walked calmly with a hand in his pocket. He couldn't remember what to think about, so he moved blankly in his own moment, free from his mind's muckraking, and left to ponder only the present if he so chose – which he did not. He turned Huntington Street's south bend with a stunning pivot, and headed for his home.

He reached his apartment door, unlocked it, and threw his keys on the table. The red light blinked on his answering machine, indicating a new message, so upon entering he walked straight to it and pressed its button.

A voice came on saying, "Hi Page. This is Rose calling, your mother's caretaker. I'm afraid I have some bad news."

Page was bent off his bed untying his shoe laces, but all came to a stop as he listened.

"Unfortunately, your mom has passed on. It was in her sleep. I came in to wake her this morning, I'd made eggs and toast, and well – your number was the only one from the family we had here, so I assume you are the closest living relative. I hope you'll call me back with your plans. Sorry for your loss – goodbye."

The voice on the machine stopped with the clunk of a phone hanging up. Page straightened his back, dug two fingers into his thigh, and over his jeans he scratched.

"Mom," he said aloud. His pinky finger, he put in his mouth, and then shortly took it out – he brought it in front of his face and stared at it.

Page tilted his head back, took a big sniff, and sat back on the couch. His eyes watered, widened, and unfocused. The scarf Addie used to keep her hair back sat on his end table. Solemnly, he stared at it, his palm holding his chin. He picked the thing up, held it by its ends, and rubbed his thumbs over its thin black cloth. Bringing it to his face, he smelt it and came to a near cringe at the stench of its staleness. He dropped it and leaned back again. Under the scarf had been Longwell's knife. Page wasn't surprised that his friend had forgotten it there. On almost every occasion Longwell stayed over, he mistakenly left behind something. Page picked the knife up, turned it around a couple times, and then pressed gently on its tip with his finger.

The internet does amazing things. Holds plenty of uselessness, and will waste your hours. But still, it does amazing things. Page had found Sara Marie Lynn's latest address and, just as she had said, it was on Huntington Street. Getting into the building was easy, and his journey's intentions had never been as far as another face-to-face meeting, so once he had taped his note to her mailbox inside the foyer, he turned around and went back home. The note read:

They wanted nineteen, now it's twenty. There are divides in the road that you think you can stand on, but to balance you need your cane. Stand up straight, don't let your jaw drop, and just lean. Occasionally, a moment in life comes where I don't have to do that anymore. You were there for one of them. A meaningless escape. I could get my hands away from my face, look, and see things out of you. I knew what I said wouldn't mean anything, not to you, and that's true understanding. Your is a wonderful word to me when it's you. This is not something that's lovey-dovey though. I'd want to spend all this time with you, but probably couldn't stay forever. I'm just a moving-on kinda man, and it seems you're the same. I got plum to blow, and well I'm starting to think there's more to the world than just this and that. But I'd be back, we're beings of habit, and I find you all too tingly to cut off, Sara Marie. I have your name, and I will see you.

A knock came on Page's door and it startled him. Stuck on the couch, leaning off it crunched, he waited for a second one. It came and he got up, opened the door, and found the building's landlord waiting on the other side – he'd already begun to walk away.

"Oh, good. I was worried you wouldn't be here," the landlord said, turning around.

"Yeah, no I'm here," Page said slowly. "Come on in."

He did and said, "I got your message, and you certainly can rent the apartment for another two months. We've got nobody in line for it right now."

Page followed him into the kitchen.

"Oh, good," Page replied. "I can give you the rent in cash now, just give me a second to go get it."

"Can't say no to that," the landlord admitted, his smile snuggling tight and deep into his face.

Page headed for his bedroom.

"So you must like it here then, huh?"

"Yeah, it's nice," Page called from the other room. "You know, quiet, but still has got some hustle too."

"Yep. Not many places like Huntington Street,"

the landlord agreed. Pulling back a curtain, he looked out the window. Below was the alleyway and through it a stray cat chased after a smaller, yelping, dog. The cat reached for the dog's back feet, tripped him up, then let the dog run away again.

"Hmm," the landlord observed and looked back for Page, but he hadn't come out yet. He saw the knife sitting on the kitchen counter, its half-foot blade bringing an intrigued look to his face. "Hmm," he said again.

Page came back out.

"Well, I got to be on my way," the landlord announced, breaking off hastily.

"Alright, sure," Page replied, and then handed him the money.

The landlord didn't count it, but immediately pocketed the money instead – thinking it rude to distrust someone so blatantly. "Yep, basement's flooding. Does every year."

"Oh really?"

"Yep," the landlord said, shaking his head as if disappointed in himself. "Mrs. O'Reily is nearly shin deep in it. Water's coming right up from the damn ground. Been searching for that leak for years, haven't found shit."

Page nodded.

"I'm just down there like good 'ol dear Henry, hole in my bucket, and some bitch yelling at me to fix it. You should be ok up here though, huh? If the water comes this high, well, you let me know cause then we're all in for some hell."

"You got it."

"Alright, take it easy guy," he said and walked out the door.

Page was back on the couch when Addie burst through the door. She threw her bag on the recliner, and sat down next to him on the tiny couch.

"I'm so sorry, honey," she said sadly.

"Yeah, it's too bad," he replied, looking back at her shortly, and then turning away.

Addie hesitated. "She just died of old age?"

"Yep. Just being too old."

Addie nodded. "Were you close? I only ask because you've never spoken of her before."

Page nodded. "I loved her."

Addie turned her head to the coffee table. She still had her jacket on.

"How was your day?" Page asked.

Addie made a sad face. "My day was ok."

Page crossed his legs and nodded, giving a tired smile.

"Do you want anything? Or need me to get something for you?"

Page let out a slow breath, and brought his hands up to the top of his head. His hair crushing. He looked over at her and shrugged. "No."

She threw her keys onto the coffee table.

"Oh, here's your hair wrap thingy. You'd left it here," he said leaning over to get it from the floor.

"Oh. Thank you," she cautiously replied.

Page dropped it on her lap. "Not to be rude but, I'd kind of like to be alone right now. You know, I just don't want to be around anyone."

"Oh, ok."

She picked her keys back up then stood. "I'll knock next time," she said. He wasn't saying anything back, so she turned and left. He let out another deep breath.

An hour later he was standing outside Giselle's door. His chin up, and he was itching his neck. She opened her door, and he didn't leave for hours – giving her the whole night and the early hours of the next day to properly heal him. He fell asleep first.

The afternoon drifted along in an overcast. The sun, despite its best intentions, had neither the course nor the capacity to come through at any point of the day – the clouds had no budge. Around six in the evening, Page turned over the lock and had to nudge Giselle's door unstuck to swing it out of its frame. Under one of the stairway arches, she leisurely leaned her shoulder against the cold stone. Her hips and bare legs curving the length of her, she silently waved.

Page was heading for the Fish Kettle. He moved in a thorny demeanor. Cliff was even with him, across the street with a camera held up, taking snapshots of Huntington Street – its frequenters, its humble keepers, its padded boundaries. Upon noticing Page on the street's other side, Cliff zoomed-in for a portrait shot of him. He snapped the picture, and then said this though nobody heard him say it, "Finally, my Richard Avedon. But is it the man covered in mud or the refined city dweller? A young bourgeois member leaving his scene, the celebrity, or the naked body tattooed? Perhaps, the American drifter. A psychedelic – yes it must be psyched – just look, it carries a potential for over-bubbling. It is mean, it is dirty, and it is freak. I can't stand it, I love it, and I think it loves me back. Bland, uninterested but tempted. No room for innocence, no need for atonement."

The next afternoon, Sue-Ellen and Addie were back at the coffee shop. This time Sue had nothing in her hands, and she was the one who had asked Addie for the talk. Sue's hair was neatly primmed, she had gotten it cut a little shorter than usual and all of it fell in its predisposed place, while Addie had loosely tied hers together. Bundled, it fell around her head, over her ears, and some strands looped down onto her reddened nose.

"So I have news," Sue said excitedly, her round eyes bulging.

"Oh yeah?" Addie tried to smile.

Sue held the suspense for a moment. "I'm moving to California!"

Addie paused. "Sue-Ellen, that is exciting – sudden too." She took a drag of her cigarette and out with the smoke she said, "What – what is out in California?"

"I'm going to try to become an actress."

"You act? I didn't know that."

"Well, I don't act really," Sue-Ellen answered, folding her hands, shrugging her bony shoulders, and looking down for a moment, "but that doesn't matter.

I know what I'm capable of. Acting is just the same as living – easier. They already tell you what to do."

Without any thinking, Addie replied, "Sure."

"Hey, don't worry Addie," Sue-Ellen put her hand on top of Addie's on the table. "As of right now, it's only temporary. I'm going to stay out there for at least a year to give myself enough time to try to make something of it, but no matter what happens, I'll be back around here now and again."

Addie didn't say anything.

"I just have to try this. I feel stuck in a swamp here. There's nothing left for me to do but wade until I'm all shriveled up. When you're standing in place for awhile your feet begin to hurt," she looked down and paused for a moment. "Mine do," she stopped again. "So I gotta move on, try my hand at something new."

"I think that's great," Addie answered sincerely. "I understand completely what you're saying about this swamp, and I, well, admire your uncompromising." Addie laughed to herself. "Really the only reason I'm upset is because you were the one person here I felt I could actually talk to. Say anything to. The one person who would truly listen and help me. I don't know what it is about you, I don't know that you were ever right with any advice you ever gave me, but I know it doesn't matter. There was something about just sitting here with you. Drinking tea. Or coffee. It's the way you say things to me, it makes me feel better."

"They have phones in California too. I'll call.

And what about Page? He's smart, caring, seems like he may listen, can't you talk to him about things?"

"He has a lot going on right now," Addie sucked her cigarette. "His mom just died."

"Oh, no. From what?"

"Just being old."

"I see."

"So yeah, understandably, he's tough to talk to right now."

"How's he taking it?"

"I guess ok. Though I can't say I'm a hundred percent sure. On the outside, he acts like he's taking it well. Just moving along. But I know him. The inside of his head must look like a Jackson Pollock painting. It's somehow together, but the paint's been thrown around everywhere. His insides are wet and still dripping."

"Hmmph," Sue-Ellen took a sip of tea. "I'm sure if you brought a problem of yours up to him though, that he'd listen, understand and try to help."

"Yeah, maybe," Addie stopped mid-thought. She averted her eyes, "I don't know how much I like him anymore anyways."

"What?"

"He doesn't care as much for me as he used to, I know that. He doesn't always want my company, and when he looks at me, all I feel is dead. I see that face and I know I used to love him. I used to, I used to, everything's I used to. I don't feel shit anymore!" Her voice suddenly rose, startling Sue-Ellen. "I get up to leave the room and nobody even budges. Not Page, not anybody. Nobody gives a shit. I'm lucky if they look up to say goodbye to me." She took a deep breath to try and calm herself. "I'm alone, Sue-Ellen, alone."

"No," she replied soothingly. She tried to put her hand on Addie's again, but she slipped it out from underneath. "You are not alone, my dear. Loneliness is always self-inflicted."

"It's beyond loneliness. I'm numb to loneliness. I'll die and months later someone will realize they haven't seen me for awhile, and they won't even think to ask where I've been. It'll just be, 'oh, haven't seen that Addie girl for awhile, hmmm. Guess I'll go on with my day'. I'm perpetually forgotten."

"Well, Addie, everyone is eventually forgotten. We pass, and maybe someone keeps thinking of us, but then they die, and nobody's here to think about you anymore. It doesn't always even have to be so drastic. Who was your first ever friend? You've forgotten her! Now you may not love Page, he may not love you, and that's fine. There's always someone else to find, there are more people than you know. But you can't go around expecting to never be forgotten."

Addie put a cigarette in her mouth, lit it, and sucked. Its burning end receded quickly, and she let out a billow of smoke while looking out the window. "Just forget about all this."

Sue-Ellen leaned back from the table, wishing she didn't believe that she had not reached her friend.

"I don't know, it's all just a part of life, right? Nobody ever said this was going to be easy. These problems, they're just me, they're mine, everyone has their own," she said, ashing. "I'll learn to live in this," she said as if she'd disgustingly satisfied herself.

Addie stood outside Page's door. She stared at her anchored feet while her shoulders swayed with indecision. Page opened the door with a small bag of trash in his hand. He stopped and looked at her.

"Were you going to come in?"

"Yes."

"Still you don't knock, huh?" He didn't listen for the answer, but dropped the trash bag outside the door and walked inside. "What you been doing?"

"Just being with Sue."

"Oh yeah?" he asked as he crashed down into his recliner. "What's the word from Sue?"

"We just talked – about life."

"Life? There's a good thing to talk about." He readjusted himself with a grunt and shut his eyes.

"She's moving to California. Wants to become an actress," Addie said throwing her jacket onto the couch.

"That's nice," Page said without opening his eyes.

"Yeah." Her word had hardly escaped her before she collapsed into Page's lap.

He thought about it for a moment, her black

hair draped over his arm, and her eyes already settled shut. He let out a sigh and relented. In the chair, they slept through the night.

The next day around two or so, Page came back to his apartment. He shut the door behind him and stopped just inside. The chair he had spent the night with Addie in was straight ahead of him. He stood still for a moment, collected thoughts, and put a hand through his hair – in the other he clutched his set of keys. His forearm pulsing, with all he had left, he threw the keys against the wall. They hit and dropped to the floor just as he did.

He'd woken up alone in the chair, had a morning coffee, gone about his day, and just around noon went over to see Addie. She was dead when he got there. Page looked her over for a moment from the doorway, blood dried on both her arms, and he turned and wandered back for home – weary and worn out.

There were no thoughts coming to him as he sat with his back up against the door. Blank and void, Page squinted his eyes as if focused. His heartbeat raced, and he tapped his fingers to its pulse on the wooden floor.

"Hope that did it for her," he said aloud, nearly laughing. Tears began to fall.

He slowly collapsed onto his side, one arm

underneath him and the other wrapping around his head, his feet lightly beating the door behind him.

There is no feeling like desertion. Desolate, and left out for nothing. Page picked himself up, sulked over to his chair and fell into it. Upon realizing it was where they had slept the night before, he groaned, rolled off, and was back down crumpled on the floor.

The blade cut sharply atop the skin of the neck. Flicked up, and the same motion sliced again.

"Nothing beats a close shave," Longwell remarked from the barber's chair.

"You got that right," Colander agreed from the chair next to him.

Both faces were piled up with shaving cream, their bodies covered by white smocks, and with glistened razors the barbers were able to work swiftly through their young stubble.

"We're gonna look sharp, real sharp," Longwell delighted. "Today is the day, my friend. You got a worry? I can't think of one."

"I see open skies, the sun, maybe a cloud or two, but ones that are there just to make it all look pretty," Colander said laughing. "No, it's hard to worry when you know you just have to fall into the money."

The barbers finished at nearly the same time. They took off the smocks, and the two young men stood up out of their chairs, each checking himself in the mirror.

Colander ran a palm against the smooth feel of nothing on his face. "Mama, come wipe my baby's bottom," he said.

The two left the barbershop and stood outside on the sidewalk.

Longwell took an embellished sniff of the air. "You smell that, Colander?"

"I don't smell shit. I'm filled up the nose."

Longwell let out a dry cackle. "Me too. But, oh baby, I can still smell money! Money baby, oo-wee! Come on, let's go get Page." He motioned with his hand for Colander to follow him down the street. "Let's do this thing."

"Can we get food before we leave? I want a burger," Colander asked while following.

"We'll get it on the way," Longwell replied impatiently.

"Well why don't we just get it now?"

"Because I wanna get on the road."

"But then we'll just have to stop –"

"Sh-u-t u-p."

Page stood over Addie's car, looking in through the driver's window. She'd parked at the south corner, right near the Fish Kettle. Two young men whom Page knew from here and there walked by in mid-conversation.

"How does New Guinea have anything to do with this?" Cliff loudly questioned, and the two young men stopped walking.

"Cliff, man, come on. It's a perfect model. Jared Diamond tells us the reason Europeans were able to colonize New Guinea and not the other way around, was simply because of the technologically advanced resources the Europeans had at their disposal. Guns, motherfucker. They had the ships and institutions to organize the trip over, as well as to carry out the whole colonization process. You know, they had the motherfucking guns, but also the paperwork to really grab them by the balls. New Guineans are there with their bow and arrows, sticks, and are throwing rocks at the giant ship that's approaching the beach. BOOM! Fucking cannon takes out half of them, you know? The last guy, just on the half of those that didn't get maimed, looks over at his brothers, dead and bloody, and what's his reaction?"

"I'm gonna kill those motherfuckers," Cliff answered.

"You're damn right. And then he gets taken out by the second shot from the cannon. Now, there are also those that don't want to fight, want to solve the problem peacefully, and the Europeans hand those guys the paperwork. Fancy treaties. Agreements that apologized for killing all those guys back there on the beach, lip service, and then here sign this and we'll start helping each other out. And the treaties aren't giving the New Guineans shit, I mean they don't have to! They just showed the people, 'you want to go against us? You don't like the peaceful agreement that we're trying to serve you? You don't like our demands? Yeah, remember those motherfucking cannons? BOOM! These New Guineans, man, I mean what the fuck are you going to do?"

"I'll tell you what we should do," Cliff said quickly, and the two started walking again.

Page fixed the hat on his head. He watched the two young men walk off behind him, and turned back to Addie's car to stare some more. His eyes were struck by the sun's sharp reflection in the window.

The weather outside was beautiful. The every-so-often autumn day that pops into the season's erratic schedule, with neither warning nor merit, is welcomed always by everyone. What it heralded on the day in which the three were to carry-out the man formerly known as Cortez's arranged deal is up for any kind of treadmill analyzing. The sun was producing heat, the wind cutting, and the royal blue sky's aura was out to soothe. A monster-sized cloud drifted between Page and the sun. He looked up at it thankfully, adjusted his coat, and stared at the window much more easily now.

No there's nothing out there for me today. No swing, no bike, no lazy hike. No, not today. Not yesterday neither. I sat in a chair, let the sun fall down, and it wasn't even that pretty. The day before, while standing in the door, I called, "Whitty? – Whitty? Come on inside, the air's a-bleeding, and you getting too skinny." No, no outside for me today. There's danger lurking at every corner. Things are frying, and I'm a-lying. It's not my fault! Who are you people? No one said nothing bad about someone passing away in their rocking chair, sitting for their whole stay. No, not today, I don't want one sun's ray.

Longwell and Colander were soon at the car.

Longwell knocked on the back window, behind the driver's seat. "You look like a fucking bum in there, what are you doing sitting in the back?"

Page put the pen in his coat-pocket. Next to it was Longwell's knife. He turned the knob to bring the window down. "You drive. I don't know where this place is."

Page kept a hold of the unlatched middle belt in one hand, and let his other hang off the door's armrest. The belt remained strained for the entire car ride. Longwell drove, and light conversation came between only him and Colander. They had stopped at a burger place, and Colander stoutly pondered over his burger before eating.

"What's wrong with it?" Longwell asked.

"Nothing. I got to wash my hands. Germs," Colander replied.

"Germs – what a scam that is," Longwell started, one hand on the wheel, the other in his fries. "You think greasy burger-boy washed his hands after scratching his crotch?"

Colander peered wearily at his meat between the buns.

"The anti-bacterial soap industry, that's who's behind the germ lie. These microscopic tiny bugs crawling around, just waiting for you to eat something without washing your hands. Crawl inside and make you sick. Come on," Longwell said dismissingly.

"Your scientific knowledge is real – it's real

good," Colander responded, looking over at his friend.

Longwell laughed. "Hey, well," he said shrugging. He decided not to finish, and dug a couple fries out.

"I just like to wash my hands before I eat," Colander said. "It's more a mental thing."

Page's expression hadn't changed, and he kept watch of the outside passing. Gone were the dulled bricks of Huntington Street, and now neon plastic signs ran along the roadside, introducing the businesses, and following corporate's wishes. Traffic lights stopped them often.

"Aren't you hungry?" Longwell asked.

"Yes."

"Well then what the fuck? We're not going to be stopping anywhere just so you can wash your hands."

Colander said nothing.

"You can't get over your stupid mental hump? Now I know that germs exist and that they can cause bodily harm. But I couldn't even count how many times I've eaten without washing my hands and not gotten one bit sick. I mean I'm not going to rub my hands in a pile of shit and then eat something. But I'm not going to sit here like a sap, let my burger get cold, my stomach go hungry, all because I'm afraid of some bullshit germ getting me sick."

"Just eat your own, leave me alone! If I don't want to eat mine, it has nothing to do with you,"

Colander replied.

Longwell took a purposefully oversized bite of his burger and let the excess meat, bun, lettuce, and tomato fall out of his mouth and litter the front seats. Colander shook his head, turned to look out the window, and watched a billboard for Pete's Laundro-Matic go by. It was a picture of a clean looking Pete smiling, a sparkle coming off his teeth, and soapy bubbles all around him.

For a time, more light conversation passed between the two sitting up front. They had driven beyond the traffic lights, and now rode a country highway – fellow drivers being scarce, neon signs giving way to trees.

"Hey, what's with you back there, Poopy-Pants?" Longwell asked of Page.

"I'm fine."

Longwell passed a car on its left side at a fast speed, leaving it well behind.

"Where is Addie anyways?" Colander asked.

Page hesitated. "She's gone – gone visiting."

"Visiting who?" Longwell asked, pushing out a hiccup.

"I don't know," Page said shrugging his shoulders. He was again looking out the window.

The conversation dropped. Longwell threw the note that Cortez had written back to Page. "Hey see if you can figure out from all this mumbo-jumbo exactly where this guy wants us to go."

"Why didn't you give it to me?" Colander asked put-off. "I'm the one sitting in the navigator's seat."

"You got germs on your hands. You said so yourself," Longwell replied quite pleased with himself.

Page opened the letter and began to read. His eyes picked up momentum as he worked down the lines, his mind quickly began to race: *serene drip, chicken crossed the road, salt on potato skins? These are things I wrote in Addie's letter. The one she said she never got, that she said must have blown off her window.* His eyebrows furrowed. "That son of a bitch," he said aloud.

"What?" Longwell asked.

Colander turned around in his seat.

"Nothing," Page answered. "Are we on 56 right now?"

"I don't know, I'm hardly paying any attention. Colander and I have been yip-yapping too much."

A sign passed reading South 56.

"We're on 56 South," Colander announced.

"Ok. We need North," Page said.

Longwell warned, "Alright, u-turn."

"You better slow down," Colander said a bit shaky. He braced himself with his hands on the dashboard.

Longwell gripped the right side of the steering wheel tightly.

"You gonna slow down?" Colander asked again. "Dude, slow down."

The tires began to screech, and the car shook

the whole turn. Page got flung over in the back seat, and Colander kept himself up by pressing a hand against the window. The car skidded nearly off the road before Longwell whipped it back into the lane, adrenaline smashed, his attention re-focusing – the car sped down the road in the opposite direction.

"Oo-baby!" Longwell shouted to the roof.

"What the fuck was that for?" Colander asked, still a bit fearful.

"Oh come on. There were no cars around. Who the hell cares?" he responded. "Just having a little fun, ok buddy? You stay with me."

Page said nothing and brought himself back up in the seat. A twinge between his ribs startled him. He opened the jacket and saw on the pocket's lining a splotch of red, one slightly larger expanding on his shirt. He un-tucked, pulled the shirt up and saw a cut in his skin. The knife tip had cut through his coat pocket, but the stab was not deep and would cause him no trouble besides the initial sting. He let the coat fall back down, the knife's blunt end striking his ribs twice in the dropping momentum – he sighed and focused again on the road.

Longwell brought the car to a quick stop, just short of the grey barn's sliding door. Colander and Page looked out their windows to see the hilltop, while Longwell flung open his door, scrambled from his seat, and came to the car's front. The other two slowly pulled themselves from their seats. The dirt road crackled under each step as they got out of the car. Longwell looked from the hill, to his friends, and then back at the hill.

"Well, it would seem we're here," he told them.

"Yep," Colander agreed.

Page remained quiet.

Longwell made the first move towards the hill-bottom, and the others followed suit.

The farm was not an old-time relic. It was still working. There were sheep, cattle, and pigs, all kept in separate pens scattered around the base of the hill. A hardly laid trail of footsteps was in-between the cattle and the pig pens and continued up beyond the fences, the rest of the livestock, and out to the open hillside. Steeper in slope the hill rose, the increase coming quickly. The grass grew longer near the top, the sun beat unguarded, and the chore of ascension became much more than any of them had anticipated – Longwell suffered especially. When afternoons are spent in smoky bar houses, there is little need for lungs to practice their expanding, consequently, Longwell's were out of training, and his breathing pinched. He was nearly bent over with his hands dragging through the grass tips, huffing and sneezing, complaining every inch.

"Why the hell couldn't we have met at the bottom of the hill? Better yet, in the barn," Longwell breathlessly spat, hunched over, so it looked as if he were speaking straight into the ground.

Neither answered him. They were both in midst of their own physical struggle, and were thrift with their breath.

"Maybe this is telling me," Colander paused for air. "That I should work out more."

Longwell began to laugh and it turned into a wheezing cough. "Don't make me laugh," he shot out. "I'll drop down dead."

The three finally made it to the top. Longwell and Colander collapsed on their bellies, sucking in the clean country air, and regaining their breath. Page sat on his butt, his chicken legs pushing up boney knees; he looked down to the hill's bottom, far away, and lit a cigarette. He took the hat from off his head.

Longwell looked at his watch. "Ok, we got here fifteen minutes early. That should be enough time," a hiccup broke his speech, “to make some sort of recovery. Hopefully, they won’t be early.”

Page blew the smoke down into his lap.

After the recovery, all three were standing up. Page dropped his cigarette into the grass. With his boot toe, he rubbed it out. A crow made an unsettling caw as it flew low overhead, annoyed, Page grimaced at it. Colander looked at the tree line behind them, and turned forward with a bit of unease. Longwell stared forward. The three stood waiting atop the half-moon hill. Page shoved his hands into his pockets, Longwell stood with his arms crossed, resting on his belly, and Colander stopped smiling.

"Let's do this and get the fuck outta here," Longwell said.

"Yep," Page coolly agreed.

"I got the creeps, but – I don't know – there is something nice about it out here. The way the trees sway with the wind maybe."

Page spit on the ground and fastened a hand to his hip.

It was a scene. The three men standing in line hilltop. The sun up and the wind moving. The figures loomed, and the sight of them was captured by a hill-bottom onlooker. Heel to toe in mud, chewing on his food, and looking up at the three men, thinking them rude, most definitely unwelcomed and intruding. It was a pig and he was chewing his grass sloppily. His memory of the three faded as his eyeballing ceased. A snotty sneeze blew out his nose, and the pig shook his head. He lazily crossed the grass area of the pen, finished a chew, and then dropped his gorged body down quite unceremoniously into brown muddy slop.

From the hilltop, the three could see a car coming down the road. A trail of dirt followed it. None of the men said a word. Longwell adjusted his weight from side-to-side impatiently, while Colander passed the time still watching the trees move. Page relentlessly tried to piece together the connection between Cortez's note, his own, and these approaching men. He wasn't able to come to much. Each lead came to a stop as he realized there was no going further with such little knowledge he had of these people. He knew nothing about them, not a motive, not a face. He felt as if he were being picked on by ghosts. His thoughts drifted and he looked over at Longwell, biting his lip.

"Addie's a good girl," Page told him. "You shouldn't talk to her like you do."

"What?" Longwell asked.

"You heard me," Page answered and turned back forward. "She's a good girl," he affirmed.

The SUV pulled-up and parked next to Addie's car. Two front doors opened as did a back, and three men got out. The man from the back eyed the other car as he shuffled by it.

The three took the same path between the pigs

and the cows. They too began to hunch over against the hill's slope.

"Look at them, barely able to make it up either. This fucking hill," Longwell said laughing.

When the other men finally made it to the top, they were just as out of breath as Colander, Longwell, and Page had been. Longwell, however, gave them no time to recover.

"Alright, you got the stuff or what? Let's have it," he shortly demanded.

"The stuff?" one of them asked in quick breaths. "You're giving us," he hesitated, "the stuff."

Page looked at Longwell, who now stared down the man who'd just spoken. On both sides radiating was obvious concern.

"Which one of yous is the little poet?" the man across from Colander asked.

The three friends looked each other over.

"I am," Colander said stepping forward, though he clearly was not.

Page looked at his friend in surprise and countered the inquiring man, "Why are you asking?"

The man turned from Colander and now looked at Page. He took a step back – eyeing both of them.

"So you don't have anything to give us?" Longwell asked.

"No," said the man across from him, shaking his head. He had on his own look of concern.

"Which one of yous been diddling through the

girlies?" asked the man across from Page.

"This guy right here," Colander answered, pointing to himself. "I'll take any girl I want."

Page's eyes bulged from under the brim of his hat.

"Why are you asking all these questions?" Longwell asked.

The opposing men said nothing, and they kept an eye on Colander, whom they'd been duped to assume was the poet diddling girlies. "Yous the guy that killed Donny then, huh?"

Page and Longwell noticed all three men were staring at Colander, and Colander stared straight back.

"Yeah, I killed Donny, his fucking grandmother too," Colander answered. "Are you the bastards spying on me? Stealing my forks?"

Longwell shot Colander a confused look. He'd not remembered the previous conversation in the Fish Kettle about Colander's missing fork.

"No," one of the men responded.

"That's good, 'cus you better not be."

Page stared down the guy across from him.

"What's going on here? Give us the guy, and then we gets the fuck out of here!" Page's man yelled.

Page bit down the tip of his tongue.

Longwell had figured it out too, and didn't waste another moment before punching the man closest to him across the face.

Upon his lead, Page did the same to his guy.

Colander took two steps back, as did the man across from him.

A full-on fight broke out between Page, his man, and Longwell and his. None of them were much of a fighter, so it wasn't going to last too long. Bad punches and cowardly blocks.

Page's face tightened as his counterpart had him weakly by the neck. He reached into his coat pocket and pulled out the knife. The other man never saw it coming, and Page could feel the grip falling limp around his neck as the knife in his hand jabbed in and out of the man's stomach. The stabbed man doubled over, stepping back from Page. The man stared at his bloody hands for a split second before Page grabbed him by the belt, around his back, and flung his weakened body down the hill.

Nobody else noticed.

Colander was bigger than his guy, but the two were shadow boxing, shuffling around each other, neither ready to really fight.

"Oh, you're pretty," Colander taunted with his fists up.

"Yeah, you'll see just how pretty I am."

"Oh, yeah? Good. I love a pretty bitch."

Longwell landed a money-punch, and his guy crumbled to the ground. He shook the pain out of his fist, and looked over at Page standing still, no adversary in sight, a knife in his hand and blood falling off its blade – running all down his forearm. Page stood motionless, his knife out and ready.

"Oh, shit," Longwell said, and then turned and saw the stabbed man rolling down the hill. "What the hell was that?" he asked Page, right up in his face.

Page's eyes did not acknowledge him.

Colander stopped his footwork and brought his fists down. His guy did the same, and they both looked from Page to the man tumbling down the hill.

"Colander run," Longwell said.

And he did.

"Come on. We gotta get the fuck out of here!" Longwell said grabbing Page by the elbow.

Page spun out of Longwell's clutch, throwing his arm back, and then righting his coat sleeve. The two made a moment's worth of eye-contact, and Longwell could not tell if Page's face wore a vacancy that annulled or one that was empty. Longwell glared in – Page dropped the knife and took off after Colander. Longwell watched them run down the hill, and then turned to the guy who Colander had been fighting.

"Hey, no hard feelings, huh? Donny was," Longwell hesitated, as he had no idea who Donny was, "always a prick." He shrugged.

The man, bewildered by what had happened, turned his look to fear as Longwell began to approach – portly, round, and stout.

Longwell hounded him. The man tried to back away, but could not make it far before Longwell punched him across the chin. He fell right down, not really wanting to get back up. Longwell shook his fist again, satisfied, he turned and began to run down the hill. The stabbed man's body was rolling in front of him, and as he ran by, Longwell kicked the man's face, sending blood from his mouth, and changing the course of his fall.

"Oh, baby!" he shouted, feeling the rush, and lumbering the rest of the way down the hill.

At the hill's bottom, the pig sat in the mud disturbed, first by Colander and Page running by, then Longwell's passing heavy breath, and finally again when a stiff body came rolling underneath the wooden beamed fence. The fat pig tried to get on its feet, move out of the way, and avoid the intruder but he was not quick enough, and the body took the feet out from beneath him. Tripping the pig over – the man's loose neck whipped his face into the mud.

Longwell jumped into the driver's seat with the car already running. Colander had started it, and he and Page were in the same seats they had been in before. Longwell threw the transmission into reverse, floored it, and backed straight out from the cloud of dust.

"Those were some stupid-ass bastards," Longwell said, still somehow pleased with the meeting's impromptu outcome. "Who comes to a place ten minutes late trying to kill somebody, totally out of breath, and asking all sorts of obvious questions?"

"Kill him?" Colander asked surprised. "How do you know they wanted to kill Page?"

"They wanted to take him at least. What else would they have wanted? An autograph?"

Colander thought for a moment. "Then what was this whole deal about? You said we were just handing something off to them, but they never gave us anything to give. No package, no money. And the other guys, they had nothing either."

"Well, if it was me they wanted, then I certainly was brought there to be handed-off," Page calmly stated. He looked dead at Longwell.

"We were setup," Colander said.

Longwell glared back. He re-positioned his grip on top of the steering wheel, stuck his other hand out the window, and took his eyes off the road for a moment. "Know of any reason why someone would want to do this to you?" he asked into the rearview mirror.

Page lowered himself in his seat. He thought for a moment. "No," he said. "I have no idea why someone would want me dead. I suppose the person to ask would be this mob guy. Which reminds me actually, that son-of-a-bitch used things in his letter to you that I put in a note to Addie – a note she told me she never got. I put it on her windshield. The car was parked on Huntington Street."

There were a couple minutes of silence. Colander realized the car Page's note had been stolen from was the very one they drove in. He became spooked in the coincidence. He let his eyes take a look over the constraints of the car's interior, and kept from touching anything inside it. Since mentioning Addie, Page's wounds had re-opened, and he'd sunk back into himself.

"I don't know how good an idea it would be to go back to this mob guy, asking him questions if he wants you dead," Colander said.

Page itched the end of his nose with his thumb.

Colander glanced at Longwell, then back to the

passing road.

"But then there's the matter of the money," Colander added.

"I know," Longwell acknowledged. "This job might be a botched one. I mean, Page fucking stabbed that guy. You crazy bastard," Longwell said shaking his head with a slight smile. "That was not part of the plan, and I don't think Cortez's business partner on the other end of the deal is really going to appreciate you doing that." He briefly looked out his window. "Of course, if it was all just a ploy to get you, then I don't think they have any grounds to be so upset about you laying one of their guys out."

"Turn around, we'll go back and see if the guy I stabbed has anything to say. He's bound to still be there, right?"

Nobody said anything.

"He may be dead," Colander realized.

Nobody said anything.

Longwell let out a tired groan. "Alright then. You wanna go ask a dead guy what he knows about all this? Hold on." he brought his hand to the wheel and jerked it in the same fashion that had sent them on the u-turn before. Page got thrown across the backseat again, and Colander held the handle above the door tightly as the car careened across the empty lanes. Turning back to the farm, Longwell lamented, "I can't believe I forgot beers for the road."

"Do you think he's dead?" Colander asked while standing over the motionless body, its face still stuck in the mud. The darkness of the slop covered any hints of the red escaping blood, but there was a sporadic trail of crimson running down the hillside. Longwell grabbed a hand-full of the man's hair and pulled his face out of the muck. Out came his mug and in went a suck of air. Startled and with a gasp, Longwell back-peddled a few steps before falling backwards into the mud. The stabbed man's face fell back in too. "Holy shit," Longwell said from his backside.

Colander hurried to the stabbed man and turned the body over.

The man was clearly near death, but still miraculously breathing. His face was wet from perspiration, undoubtedly pig piss, and all the other vile liquids that combine into pigsty mud. His eyes were blinking shut and open.

Page leaned over, and pulled him up by the shirt collar. "Who the fuck are you? And why the fuck are you trying to kill me?"

The man made a gurgling sound, his face miserably straining. Page dropped him back into the mud.

Colander looked around to make sure nobody saw them. The car the other guys had arrived in was gone now. Thinking their man surely dead, and not wanting to be around when the body was discovered, they had left. These were not well trained mob men. Colander was worried about the owners of the farm too though.

"What's he saying?" Longwell asked, sticking his head in.

"I don't know, he's just choking on his own vomit, blood, shit, and whatever else." Page wiped the filth from his hands onto his pant leg. He looked down at the man he had stabbed and became mad again. "How do you know Addie?" he asked through clenched teeth, picking the man up. The man's eyes were open, his pupils floating aimlessly, but his mouth remained shut. Page dropped him again.

"He doesn't know shit," Longwell said. The man spit blood at Longwell's shoes – not entirely on purpose. "What the fuck was that?" he shouted and hurried in a kick to the man's ribs.

"Hey!" Page came back, pushing his friend away. "What are you doing?"

"I'm sorry," Longwell responded, catching himself. "It's just – he fucking spit on me."

The man's eyes closed and body stilled. Page stood up from him, cursed once, and walked away while lighting a cigarette. Through his pursed lips, he called back, "Well now you're right, he's not going to tell us shit." And after taking the cigarette from out of his mouth, he said, "Just let him die."

Longwell bent over the man. One after another low wheezing breath escaped his whitening lips, and the man's dying eyes swelled from under the brow.

"Alright buddy," Longwell said standing up. He stuck his foot underneath the man, lifted, and flipped the body back to belly-down. Then with his foot on the back of the man's head, Longwell pushed his face into the suffocating gunk, ear deep. He casually gave the farm setting a once-over. "It's disgusting out here," he said. Another groan came, and the air pushing out of the man's lungs bubbled up in the slop.

Page and Colander wandered outside the pigpen. The wind came with the smell of fall in it, rushing through and making the leaves blow. Colander once again watched, standing with his legs spread wider than his hips, and his arms wrapped at the chest. Some leaves stuck to the trees while others blew off. Page sucked down his cigarette, wallowing in the weight that had been piling on him all day. The wind made his cigarette burn too quick for his liking, and in one particularly big gust, he had to hold the top of his hat to keep it from coming off.

After the mud stopped bubbling, Longwell returned the dead man over to his back.

"He's dead," he announced to the others.

Both turned and started walking back. They

stepped over the pen's fence and met Longwell at the lifeless body. It was obvious the man was dead.

"Alright, let's get outta here," Page said quietly. He flicked his cigarette into the mud.

"I don't know why we even came back here in the first place," Longwell said.

Longwell slammed the door shut and took off down the sidewalk in long, determined, steps, as if he were a man who'd been wronged, and actually had the good mind, the strength, and the backing to go and give the wrongdoer a piece of his mind.

"Fuck this guy. He's a faggy haired, skinny-little, shit. And if he thinks he can throw *this guy*," he pointed his thumb at himself, "out the door for the dogs to come chew-up, well, I'll tell you first, but he's got another thing coming to him too. I let the $50,000 go out of a business negotiation tactic, not because I'm scared of him."

Colander and Page moved slightly slower than their friend. A casually dressed man followed behind them. He wore a pointy crew-cut, was well in shape and his clean look was near cause for suspicion in such an un-kept hair, un-shaven face, and generally un-groomed type of neighborhood.

"Longwell," Colander said. "Are you crazy? He's a mob boss. This guy tried to have Page killed. Who knows, maybe he expected me and you to be whacked too."

"Even better. We'll bust in and say, 'look – look

fucker. We're still alive.'"

"And then he's gonna shoot you in the head!" Colander deduced with an arm raised. "Plus, where are you going to find this guy? You have no idea where he is."

"Yeah, I don't think this is a good idea," Page added.

"We'll go to the backroom of that diner we first met him in. The 24-hour whatever," Longwell answered.

The crew-cut man pushed an earpiece around with his finger. He quickened his step to stay close behind the three.

"And what, you're just going to kick down the door? They will shoot you twenty times before you get the chance to even call him a faggy haired, skinny-little, shit."

"I probably wouldn't call him that," Longwell answered as if he were under control.

"Don't do this, Longwell," Page said again.

Longwell stopped walking and turned back to his friends.

The crew-cut man had to abruptly stop his shadowing. With no newspaper to provide a cover, the man turned to face the road, and as if he'd not been following the three at all nor even acknowledging them, he stared blankly into the empty street. With a nervous eye, he shot quick glances toward them.

"Look," Longwell began. In his peripheral he

noticed the crew-cut man giving them looks. "Who the fuck is this guy?" he asked gesturing towards the crew-cut man. He lumbered past his friends and glared at their nervous shadow. The crew-cut man shot a glance at the approaching fat man, swallowed a few times, and then maintained his stare at the street.

"Are you following us?" Longwell asked the man, pushing him at the chest into a building.

"Me? No."

"What do you got in your ear there?"

"Nothing."

"Let me see that," Longwell brought his hand up to the man's ear, but Crew-cut knocked it away.

"What are you doing?" Page called over.

"This guy was following us," Longwell accused the man to his face.

"I was not." The man shook his head.

Colander and Page walked over concerned. Colander became tough again, he patted Page in the stomach to tell him to hold back, and he continued alone towards the shadow.

"You the guy stealing my forks?"

The crew-cut man backed-up further against the building.

Longwell looked to Colander, "What is all this fork business?"

With the two momentarily distracted, the crew-cut man made a run for it. Mid-sprint, he pulled a walkie-talkie from his pocket, "It's a go, all-out breach, all-out!" he shouted into it. As the man approached Page, he began to give some jukes. Page crouched down low with his arms out, but his weight got going the wrong way. In a last ditch effort, Page stuck his leg out, but could only briefly trip the man up as he went by. Crew-cut stumbled, but regained his balance with a hand to the ground. Down the street, he disappeared.

"What the hell was that?" Page asked the other two, softly putting himself down onto the ground, his leg still sticking out.

Just then, up and down the street, law enforcement agents broke out of their everyday disguises and drew their guns. Immediate arrests were made, and the unsuspecting raised their hands in disbelief. More armed personnel were vehicled in from both the east and the west, and a raid on Huntington Street's residents, its ideals, and lax principles began under precisely directed measures. The drills had paid off, and the well-trained soldiers' performances exceeded all expectations of the masked policymakers. Foolishness though – foolishness, foolishness.

Ruthless, intoxicated, mathematical, elimination. Systematically bumping, chant boot pumping. Kicking and smashing. If it moved, they took it. Down, out, or gone. People running, toilets flushing. Guns firing, people ducking, dogs barking. Windows smashed and noxious gasses reeked. People inside choked, scurried out to the street, got rounded-up, cuffed, and left out to dry in the sun. Everyone got needled. They spit in their captor's face if they could. The few who had them, took out their own guns and a deadly crossfire began. Lines blurred, and the street became exactly what the policymakers thought it previously to be.

Page was ducked down, hiding in the Rickety Shell's alleyway. Crouched low, he watched as people frantically dodged around the street. He heard authoritative shouts and out of breath, up-yours, retorts. He took the moment to try and recover some comprehension. Longwell had run in the opposite direction.

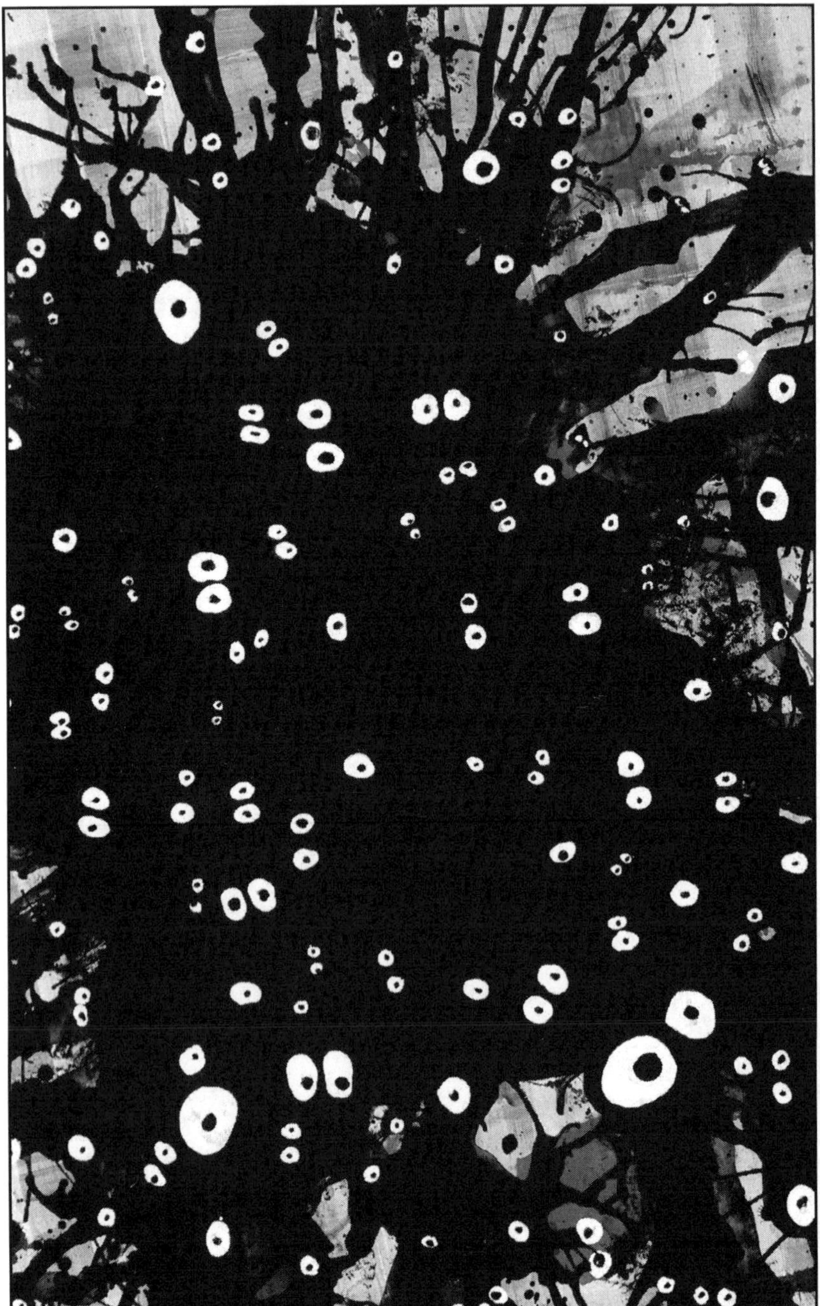

Hesitation left Colander stuck-out on the street, and with the Rickety Shell's alleyway in sight, he was held up at gunpoint. The man brandishing the gun was none other than old man Figgleman.

"Ah-ha! Mongrel! Or shall I call you by what your mother first did – Andrew Horgan. Ha! I told you I'd get you one of these days and look at us now," Figgleman said adjusting his glasses and trying to keep his hand from shaking the gun away from its target.

Colander stood with his hands up. "Who the hell are you?" he asked, the crackdown ensuing around them.

"Forgotten already, huh? I knew your mind to be weak! I'm the poor man you robbed!" His shouts made him wobble on his walker.

"I didn't rob anybody."

"How dare you insult my memory, my eyesight, my hindsight. I would of course recognize the man who took even one of my cents!" Figgleman's finger shook on the trigger.

"Look, old man, I don't know who you are, I don't know who robbed you, but there's some serious shit going down right now, and I -"

"Now you listen," he started, but he could not finish before the gun went off in one of his hand's shakes. Colander took the shot and fell dead on the ground.

From Page's hiding spot, he could see only his friend's face fall, eyes open against the pavement. A couple pairs of legs ran through the view, but they cleared in time for him to see Colander's head bounce and then become still. Page rubbed his shoulders against the brick wall behind him. Tilting his head back, he made silent faces of anguish. Any hopes of comprehension were all but stifled, muffled, and asphyxiated. The moment suddenly cleared for him, and he reached into his coat pocket for Longwell's knife, but it wasn't there, he'd dropped it on the hilltop, and he was left to think of another way to spare himself.

Figgleman dropped the gun, muttered something underneath his breath and began pushing his walker along. His slow frail movements could not get him off the street nearly quick enough, and a young resident, mid-flee with his head turned, checking his back, kicked old Mr. Figgleman's walker out from underneath him, and the old man fell hard to the ground. Again, he was laid helpless on his back. He took a deep breath. "Oh father," he lamented. "Fuck – killing a man just isn't the same as it used to be. I feel no vindication. There's no more purpose. The mourners are too busy. A man's soul has got nothing left for me. Not a laugh, not a stepping stone. Then what good is it?" Figgleman's nostrils flared. "My time, father, my time is gone."

Two officers came and stood over Figgleman. "Should we call an ambulance?" one of them asked.

"An ambulance? We would be shipping

everybody out. If the old man can make the paddy-wagon, throw him in, otherwise," he paused and shrugged, "let him die, or do it for him."

"I don't want to kill an old man."

"Then let him be," his partner said, patting him on the shoulder. "I don't think he's who we're after anyways. Hey!" he called out as he witnessed some loose, unrestrained, mischief going down. He took off down the road.

Cliff and his friend had brought chairs and other furniture down from their apartment to heave through storefront windows.

"Why are we doing this, Cliff?" his friend asked.

"Are you kidding?" Cliff bit back. He took a chair by its back and threw it through a window. "Do you need to be given a reason to breathe?" He asked looking his friend in the eye. "The respiratory system is run by the most primitive part of our brain." He grunted as he whipped another chair. "It makes sure that no matter how distracted, how consumed, or how occupied our minds are, that we still will fucking breathe!" All the chairs had been thrown, and Cliff looked around for something else. "Now pick-up the other end of this couch – help me throw it through that window."

With no knife, Page could think of no other

place to go. Outside Huntington Street he had nowhere to run to, and on it he was in the safest place he knew. Trapped in this alley, he sat in an open-door prison with an end well-guarded by thugs and formidable realities.

With a boost from his resolve, he stood up and began searching deeper into the alley for a way out through the back end. The Rickety Shell had an alley-door that the kitchen staff smoked cigarettes out of, but when Page tried it, its lock had already been turned. He banged a fist on it without much hope and gave a couple yells but nobody came. He faced the street and took a deep breath. Two steps closer to braving the gauntlet and a hand fell on his shoulder, grabbing him by the shirt collar, and yanking him through the Rickety Shell's kitchen staff door.

Page was hustled inside and pushed down into a chair. The man released Page's shirt and gave him one last downward shove though there was no further down in the chair he could go. "Now don't you think about going nowhere," the man told him, and he walked back towards the door. The room had an eerie darkness, and Page could sense other bodies. A match striked and its flame appeared. The fire rose and was snuffed out in one swoop.

"Open the shade on that window, man. Let's get a little bit of light in here," came the orders from a body that Page could not see. A guy moved from the door to the wall. He pulled back a curtain, and into the room entered the late afternoon sun. Its beams cast down in front of Page, lighting the open space where particles of dirt and dust floated. At the light's end was another chair and a pair of legs jittering.

Opposite Page was the man formerly known as Cortez. "Boo," he said and made some indistinguishable mumble followed by a laugh. He bobbed back and forth between the light and the shade. "It's me," he told Page.

The backroom was similar to the one Longwell and Colander had met Cortez in, the same type of creaky wooden chairs, the same square dimensions, a similar darkness. This time there was no table in-between. Two men kept quiet along the edge of the room, watching over the door, while the mob boss flicked at his finger nails, acting oblivious to what was going on outside and momentarily forgetting about Page.

"I don't recognize you from the meeting," he finally said to him.

"I was the one not there."

"This is the kid we set to take the rap, boss," Cortez's man explained.

"Oh," Cortez answered, a bit caught off guard. He smiled, but Page could barely see it through the darkness. "So how did the meeting go?"

"You know how it went, you set us up," Page spat back.

The reply came in a nod. "Well, maybe I should introduce myself to you," the mob boss offered. "My mother, she named me Cortez," his eyes left Page, but then quickly came back. "I never really liked that name much though. I never thought it to fit me. It was too – uhhh – too there, you know? Straight – up front. There's nowhere to hide behind Cortez."

"You'd have to conquer."

"Yeah," he agreed, and half of his face reappeared in the light. "I always figured myself more a James, Eliot, or even Ernest. I like Ernest, but how could she have ever known that, hmm? I can't blame her for that. Ernest though, that's got quite the billing. I don't know if I could live to be Ernest." He stared blankly at the ground. "But anyways, you're right. You were being used. My decision to do it was easy." He folded his hands on his lap. "One of my guys, a top earner, a brother to me. He crossed the line with one of my business associate's men. Some Donny guy. Caught sleeping with his wife. They found a love-letter. A sticky situation that there was no coming back from really. I only am telling you this because informing you soon won't matter. You won't be getting out of here alive, and well consider me telling you about this a gesture of my goodwill. Many other men die not knowing what for. For instance, the man you stabbed – he's dead."

Page didn't respond.

"Think he knows what for? No – he died in some pig's shit." Cortez thought for a moment. "But you know I've killed people. These guys have too." he said nearly smiling, amused, and pointing back at the two men behind him. He took a cigarette out. "Chalk it up to the poor sap's luck to not know why he died."

Page listened and tried to keep his cool, but he was anxiously melting.

"Anyways, my guy I was telling you about, my brother, he killed this Donny for the woman."

Recognition receded from Page's face as his deflation continued.

"So that they could be together. She asked him to." He sighed. "The things we'll do if a tit tells us to, huh?" A sullen look came to Cortez's face – he studied the young man across from him, but could not entirely figure him out. "So Donny's friends didn't appreciate that. They demanded retribution or threatened revenge. Now having people run around these streets, laying dead bodies down all over is not good for business. So I had to deliver them somebody to keep control – you. I don't turn in my brothers. And well, you sort of look like him. He's a little taller."

Page sniffed and looked at the two men guarding the door, both gun-in-hand. He looked back at Cortez, who was taking a drag from his cigarette.

"I saw my friend Colander – the tall skinny one of us three – I saw his dead body bouncing off the pavement just earlier. Right outside," Page pointed to the window. "My girlfriend, she slit her wrists this morning, also dead. My mom, three days ago, dead." He shrugged. "Death is on the move."

"Death is always on the move," Cortez responded. "Just a matter of time. It's a terrible thing."

Page leaned back in his chair. "Yeah," he said. He began to nod his head. "Yeah, you know, that's a pretty ironic thing for a guy like you to say. That death is terrible. You just told me you've killed plenty of people and you nearly started laughing, man. And then there's me, you tried to have me killed and now again – but when I told you about people who were close to me dying, you say death is a terrible thing. And you laughed – you laughed. If death is so terrible, why do you go around bringing it out?"

Cortez had no response.

"Don't you think the people you killed had others close to them too? Or me, I may have people close to me who will be upset when I die."

"You just named three people who won't be. Under your logic, you may be the most perfect man to kill," Cortez took a big swallow. "And anyways, you've never laughed at something terrible? Just even a nervous laugh? Never giggled after seeing a car crash on the TV? Never," Cortez broke for a moment of thought, "fried an ant with a magnifying glass? Held your little brother's head under water until he starts squealing? What? It's funny."

"No, I try not to laugh all that much."

"Oh," Cortez said slowly. "Well, I guess that's where you and I differ. I laugh at life all the time," he said and straightened his face. One of the men in the back let out a single chuckle, as he'd stopped watching the door and was observing his boss work. He checked himself, and looked out the window for anything suspicious.

"If you laugh too much, you risk compromising the seriousness and finites of life. At some point, you have to stop kidding yourself and realize you do care about the world you're in. You care about it more than you can anything else. Beyond caring. Without life, there's nothing for you. It'd be like trying to watch a TV show in the telephone. The show is predicated on there being a television there. Any conscious thought you have is predicated on life. It's too serious to laugh at. There's nothing beyond it," Page stopped, and his fingers grabbed his lips. He let go and crossed his arms. "Nothing at least that we could know for sure."

"That is some great shit," Cortez responded. "Inconsequential at such a moment, but you know, sounds good."

Page straightened up in his chair.

"Ok, enough chit-chat. There is business to take care of and no time," he stated. "This is how it goes. You made your mistake by coming back here. There is no choice now that we have you. If you'd not come back, we would of hardly put an effort into searching for you. We'd just give them some other guy to do. In our business, a peon is a dime-a-dozen." Cortez took a drag on his cigarette. "But you came back. We have *you*. I don't need to go find somebody else again. And I suppose there's a degree of justice that should be served. I have a responsibility. To the dead guy, the other party involved, and the business itself," Cortez looked Page in the eye. "You're an outsider who came and killed a workingman. Like everyone else, we live by standards and ideals. I have to uphold them." He took another drag, but didn't take his eyes off of Page.

Page lit his own cigarette and scratched his cheek quickly. "We came back to see you."

"What were you planning to do?"

He struggled for a response, and Cortez gave a few amused chuckles. Page chewed his thumb's fingernail. He wondered what had happened to Longwell. "I can find you another guy. Then I'll leave. Not come back. And we can pretend none of this happened. You know – make the same transition of responsibility that got thrown on me. I can find you a guy out there – no time flat."

"Ahh-ha!" Cortez pointed straight at Page with the two fingers holding his cigarette. "And that is why I laugh at life. It never earns our seriousness."

Longwell was ducked, hunkered down, and under cover. Two police officers approached, so he did all he could to hold his breath and not move. They walked by the round belly of the man, never suspecting the body sprawled out on the sidewalk to be living. Longwell opened one eye and watched the two kick down a door that had a make-shift barricade protecting it. It was a good ways down the street, and they plunged eagerly into the building's insides to gut it. Longwell rolled over and got up off the ground, brushing the dirt and debris from his pants. He hit his thigh and his hand ran over Addie's car keys, still in his pocket. He reached in and took them out, admiring his luck and closing his palm to a fist. A breath left through his nose that barely whistled. He checked up and down the street for any more officers, and nearly tiptoeing, he made his way back to the car.

Cortez planted his feet on the chair's sides and leaned into the sunlight coming in from the window. For the first time, Page could see Cortez's face entirely – chin to forehead, ear to ear. A trench etched through the skin of Cortez's cheek, and Page recognized in the man's face traces of once being a craver and crawler. The succession of years in a pit had brushed age onto his face, and now overrode any sensation he had for the days of old. But there are certain things that certain things will do to a man, and Cortez could not keep the markings off his face.

"I am going to kill you. I have to," he said dropping back into the shadow. "Now you can try to run, but I don't think you'll make it halfway to the door. You got a gun?"

"No."

"You had a knife. You still got the knife?"

"No, I dropped it on top of the hill."

Cortez looked away and nodded. "Well, kid." He stretched out his fingers and seemed to almost study them. "Some Kungfu masters are capable of channeling enough inner chi to, I don't know say, blow a whole house down maybe – with one deceptive strike," he extended his arm slowly with his palm forward, hiding half of his smile in the shadow. "Are you capable of a little deception?"

Page itched through his hair down to the scalp. If he'd known his fate on top of the hill, he figured he'd not have fought so hard.

Cortez brought his hand to his side. "Me either, that's why I got a gun," he said patting his jeans at the hip. A dust particle drifted in the light and caught Page's eye. It lingered for a moment, and then crossed into the shadow.

Longwell slipped the key into the car door and gently opened it. He slid in and turned the ignition, remaining low and hidden in the seat. His tongue edged out as he carefully pulled the car from the curb, his head just barely sticking over the steering wheel. As he slowly drove, it became apparent to him just how well Huntington Street had been ransacked. Its entrails were wrenched out and dropped on the pavement for picking through, pushing around, and for making putrid faces at.

Props from the masquerade were scattered obstacles for Longwell to guide the car through, so as to not pop a tire, stick the radiator, or bang the tailpipe. Doors had been ripped off hinges, glass shattered, and bricks once stacked into the street's buildings were now toppled over, littering Huntington's façade. Residents and frequent visitors were lined up neatly on the sidewalk, or were being pushed into the backs of trucks and cruisers to be shipped out for processing. All moaned anguish and shock. Some were slumped over parking meters, some curled up against brick, and others hung off lampposts. Those who'd stepped aside, raised a voice, or started to fight were the sacrificial.

Longwell could see they had been separated from the crowd, both in proximity and in a very general not-so-much alive sort-of way. Their blood leaked and reddened the street; though not for nothing did it fall down the drains. Sewers spread, and innocent blood has a terrible stench.

Cliff was part of those rounded up. He stood against the brick front of a building, others in line with him. Feverishly breathing out his nose, sweat came down his forehead, and he was flushed in the face. Steph had been caught as well. Again she was in a pose, her hands wrapped around the back of her hips, her neck lurching, her head forward, nose first. She had the resemblance of a turtle. Cliff ripped the glasses from his face, threw them into the street to be crushed and was then able to cool off.

Giselle was not one of those captured. Fortunately for the Lady of Huntington Street, she was out of the city on personal affairs for the afternoon, and though her house had been strip-searched, there was nothing of legal importance found, and the insides had been left virtually in-tact. The thought of her came to Longwell as he went by her house. He figured she had come out of this okay. His focus turned back to the road ahead. Out came a sigh which, like him, was heavy and ready to leave.

An officer of the law spotted this unmarked vehicle moving. "You in the car!" the man shouted. Longwell checked his rearview mirror and saw the cop fire one round from a pistol into the air. He hit the gas and took-off down the street. The officer ran after him, firing two more shots, this time at the car's tires. The south bend of Huntington Street was in the near distance, and as Longwell pushed the gas, he failed to take into account the ninety degree curve that turned the street east.

"Colander?" he asked aloud, readjusting his rearview to get another glimpse of the body he'd driven by. The passenger side of the car went over a bump.

Figgleman now was crushed and dead.

Longwell searched the mirror for a moment more before looking forward. He didn't have a chance of making the bend, yet the tires screeched as the steering wheel jerked – at first the car swerving away from the wall, but then whipping back towards it as doubts of the escape entered Longwell's mind.

The curb launched the car off the ground, putting enough air under it to send the front-end unabated and straight into the brick face of Harold's Store of All Things. The car recoiled off the wall and dropped onto the sidewalk. The windshield spider-webbed, blood on its center.

The officer slowed to a walk – no longer in a hurry. Upon reaching Addie's destroyed car, he holstered the gun, ran his fingers through his mustache, did a whistle and left the scene.

"Some nights I go to bed, lie there and think, 'was today worth it? Was it a good day?' My wife hates that. She can feel my eyes open. She says, 'yes, yes, today was good honey, today was worth every extra minute you keep those eyes of yours open,'" Cortez began to stumble his speech. "And – and 'and if I'm wrong, at least kiss me before you go,' she says," Cortez had his arms crossed, his pinky itching his bicep. He crossed a leg over while thinking of his wife, and grabbed the shin of his crossed leg. His gaze wandered out the window – to see was only the sun – and his attention came back to Page. "Today though, tonight, no need to waste any sleep."

Page's eyes did not budge from the ground. In his mind, each stab of Longwell's knife replayed.

"I've been talking too much, you got anything else to say, kid?"

Page sat silent, rubbing his thumb against each finger on his hand. He shrugged at Cortez, who patiently watched. The two men that'd been guarding the door stood behind their boss and waited on Page as well.

"What'd you steal my letter for? The images in it, you used them in your note to Longwell. Why?"

"I thought you may ask me that."

"Yeah?"

"Well –"

Page jerked, bracing his legs for a sprint out of the room. He lurched forward and only went as far as leaning off the chair before pulling his body back to it. Cortez did not move, one leg still crossed over the other, but his men pulled their guns.

"Aww, you won't kill me yet," Page said grinning, pointing his finger back and forth between the men with their guns ready. He began to laugh.

Cortez broke out in his grin, and then a few quiet snickers that naturally flushed into a full row of laughter. This only heightened Page's amusement, and his own laughing grew just as high.

In a moment that inconsequentially passed, and a movement that's fluidity was nothing less than perfect – Cortez rose – pulling the gun from his hip and firing four shots into Page's chest.

The bullets' force knocked Page's chair back and he fell, arms out and dead.

Cortez let his breath go as the gun's echo died.

One of the men took a step closer and looked over his bosses' shoulder to get a glimpse of the dead young man.

Cortez said, "I was just waiting for him to laugh".

"That's good, boss," his man told him. "We should probably get you out of here."

"Yeah," Cortez said back reasonably. "We should probably go." He turned and took his Russian mink hat off the coat stand, its warmth he thought the day's cold would warrant, and he grabbed his jacket too. One of the men opened the door to the alley, and the other checked outside to secure it. The grey trench coat Cortez wore went down past his knees, and the bottom of his jeans skidded under his boots with each stride. The curls of his hair fell out from the bottom of the fur hat, and though his attire was a little much for the unseasonably warm day, he was not bothered. In the alley he took a stride towards the street, pulling his jeans up by the belt, he stopped, and tried to get a look further down the sidewalk.

"This way, boss."

He swiveled back – unbalanced – his foot reaching back to catch him. "You're right," he said.

This next year people didn't think about last year. Last year was not a good year. It cast a giant shadow upon every one of its plebian hobblers – a shadow that's ramifications, night-time familiarities, and overarching sense of doom, drove rats to their holes, queen bees to their honey, and the grateful to their hastily dug grave. You're in the shadow! What are you gonna do? You can swing fists at the clouds, but you'll never reach the sun. Despondency, head hanging, neck cracking. It was a horrible year. Nobody wanted to be there. Get on with it, we're done. On our heels, giggling, and pleading to whoever it is that cranks these things along. Saying, "thank you, I wanna say thank you. I wanna say, thank you – I love you – but I'll be gone. When comes next year?"

1415542

Made in the USA